To Eden,

Hope you like this trip to Key West.

Ken Watt

The Big Egg

By Ron Watt

❇

To Ernie, Dos Passos, Thornton Wilder, Tennessee, Crane, MacLeish, James Leo Herlihy, James Kirkwood, Suzie DePoo, Gahan Wilson, Tom McGuane, Mario Sanchez, Ann Irvine and the others who have helped make Key West a transfixing, luxuriant cove for artists of every persuasion.

    And to all of you who love Key West,
        warts and much more.

    "We are one human family."

❇

© 2003 Airport Books LLC

ISBN: 0-9709632-1-1

Library of Congress Control Number: 2002117653

Cover Design: Kurt Roscoe
Illustration: Fred Mozzy
Layout: Francine Smith

All rights reserved under all Copyright Conventions.
Submit all requests for reprinting to:

Airport Books LLC
8227 Washington St. #2
Chagrin Falls, OH 44023

Printed in the U.S.A.

Published in the United States by Airport Books LLC,
Cleveland, Ohio.

www.airportbooks.com
www.greenleafbookgroup.com

❁

The fictional characters in this book are just that. Any resemblance to any person living or dead is purely coincidental by name or description.

❁

Table of Contents

1. The Theater Of The Weird Gets Weirder
2. Why Everything's Fine With Seamus
3. You Can Smell The Yeast On Greene Street
4. The Man Who Shoots Paint Balls
5. Some Odd Behavior At The Atlantic Shores
6. Be-Headed In The Mangroves
7. Bopping Around With Robert Cleverly
8. A Bad Night On Christmas Tree Island
9. An After-Hours Party Invitation
10. Blues In The Night
11. What Shallaha & Charla Heard At Pearl's Patio
12. Why A Boy Goes Wrong
13. A Visit To The Hospital
14. The Viscount Gets Serious
15. A Smoking Cigar
16. Finally, They Get It Down
17. Balloons Bursting All Over
18. Who Got The Viscount Out Of Jail?
19. Romance Into The Night
20. "Former Cop Arrested As Voyeur"
21. Let Them Eat Cake
22. Heidi Takes On Some Fellow Bikers
23. Heidi Slips Away
24. How Things Went Afoul At Ol' Jose Marti's Place
25. More Intrigue At The Bottom Of Duval
26. Another Day, Another Murder
27. The Police Chase Down The Viscount
28. Heidi Hamms It Up In The Bay
29. Zero Is Out Of Jail; But There Are Revolting Developments At Sea
30. Heidi And Pansy, Damsels In Deep Danger
31. A Wild Race Ensues
32. Carnage On Christmas Tree Island?

CHAPTER ONE

The Theater Of The Weird Gets Weirder

One day in Key West, not long ago, some time in the wee hours of the morning, maybe 4 a.m., a very large egg appeared beside the pier behind Mallory Square, right along the Gulf of Mexico.

The locals and even some of the "tourons" didn't at first think this odd, because, well, odd things just seem to happen on this tropical island, the lowest place on earth, latitudinally, that is still the continental United States.

It wasn't until two days later, at the break of dawn, that people started to become alarmed. That was when the big brown egg began cracking. This twenty-foot by seven-foot egg started cracking like an egg under an incubator light. But instead of hatching a giant baby chicken, the egg produced a man with a Moorish/Celtic visage, and he was wearing a blue blazer with golden epaulets, gray slacks, white bucks and a pencil thin mustachio. Out stepped the man who would change the course of Key West for the 21st century.

At 6-1 and 205 pounds, the man was not an imposing figure but he certainly was noticeable. When people asked him his name, he simply said it was Viscount. ("Vy-count, please, address me as, Vy-count and I will be pleased.")

The mystery of his origins would some day be solved but not for now. No, not until The Viscount took care of some business. What he would do would startle some and send others dispatching.

In a town of weirdos, The Viscount was over the top – figuratively and literally – for he rode about town on a nine-foot-high unicycle, which had come out of the egg with him. Sometimes he would talk to people and sometimes he wouldn't. He found Key West hotter than he expected. So in place of his gray flannel trousers, sometimes he wore gray flannel shorts. But always, always, he wore his double-breasted blue jacket with the golden epaulets and an assortment of hats, selected depending on his mood. Often he also wore a black hat with a big silver buckle around it. He wore no shirt, probably because of the heat, but always, always, he had attached to his lapel a little red poppy.

Captain Tony Tarracino, the former mayor of Key West, and the decades-long proprietor of Captain Tony's Saloon, the original Sloppy Joe's of Hemingway lore, called The Viscount "absolutely the weirdest person I have ever met in this crazy tourist town. I thought I was weird but this guy takes the cake.

"Last week he wasn't paying attention and wheeled his cycle right into our place – or sort of. Our doorframe at the top is only seven-feet high, and The Viscount comes in here at about the thirteen-foot level. Smacked his noggin real good, he did. Gave everyone a big laugh, even The Viscount himself, who wobbled over to the bar and ordered a Killian's," added Captain Tony.

Sitting at the bar next to the stool which The Viscount approached was a luscious woman in her late thirties. She was part Scottish and part Mexican and had a look about her, as did many people who had settled in Key West. This woman's name was McMary Marimba. She had the dark eyes of a Mexican and the pinkish skin of a Scot. Immediately, The Viscount took a liking to her.

"My oh my, what a handsome man," said McMary, whose green eyes twinkled and fluttered. "Where did you come from, you big hunk? I've been awaiting a guy like you for all too long."

"I have come from a distant place to enjoy the climes of Key West," said The Viscount. "It is my pleasure to meet such a fine woman as yourself, McMary, I believe I heard the bartender call you. My name is The Viscount."

"What a noble name, aristocratic, not just like plain old Bob. I hope you didn't hurt yourself running into the doorframe, Viscount. And we weren't laughing at you, we were laughing with you. You seemed to find it kind of funny yourself."

"I feel like I have already had a few Killian'ses, that's all. My noggin is a little dull from the crash, but I'll be all right, especially sitting next to such a beautiful woman as you."

McMary was wearing one of those belly halters that went down to her navel. On top she showed an ample display of femininity. She also had on cut-off Levies and was featuring an ample amount of leg as well. De rigueur in Key West. Her long brunette hair draped over her shoulders with a bit of curls on the bottom, and on top she had a bit of bangs, similar to the Betty Page look. She was seated on a stool that had Walter Cronkite's name on it. All the stools at Captain Tony's had some famous person's or some noted local's appellation on them.

The Viscount stood next to the John Candy stool. McMary liked The Viscount. He had a rakish cast about him, dark, thick, gray-streaked hair, a strong body, and today his was sporting a white sailor hat, one of the many chapeaus he fashioned. He naturally had on his double-breasted blue blazer with the epaulets, but no shirt. He had been in Key West a few days now and already was sporting a deep tan from spending his late mornings and early afternoons in the "Crow's Nest" at the bow of the Atlantic Shores' bar.

The Atlantic Shores is a moderately priced yellow

and blue motel on Atlantic Boulevard and it has a pool and long pier where people from all over the world show off their wares, that is go naked. The Viscount would not go naked but he did trim down to a black thong and often sat in the Crow's Nest, warding off the numerous young and old men who were not quite as heterosexual as he. He liked the Crow's Nest because it gave him a view of what was going on up and down the pier in front of him and to his left he could see the deck of the pool, where many more naked people cavorted.

The Viscount had little body hair, but some time ago he had some hair transplanted to his chest from the ample crop on his head, affecting a kind of Errol Flynn look, a bit of black, a bit of gray, and it looked pretty natural.

This day at Captain Tony's he had his gray flannel shorts on and on his feet were some snake-skinned Tommy Lama cowboy boots. The sweet smell of J. Crew skin bracer wafted from his jowls, as he sipped his Killian's and took in the pleasant aroma of McMary, who was wearing Sage on her neck and earlobes. It smelled inviting, he thought.

"Are you a resident of Key West?" The Viscount asked.

"Oh, yes, for twenty years now. Came here when I was 18, just looking for some fun in the sun, and like a lot of people I never left. Had a million jobs here, but for the past year I've been working on top of The

Whistle, at Eaton and Duval, in the Garden of Eden bar. You should go there. They do a lot of body painting up there. We get a lot of visitors and a lot of locals. You know the guy that plays the 'silver man' on the wharf at the sundown ceremony behind Mallory Square? He's up there all the time, likes to watch the girls get painted. It's hot up there, so most of the time I'm either topless or totally clothes-less. It's a hoot. You ought to come up tomorrow. I'll be working."

"I shall, I shall," said The Viscount, with all the vigor he could muster. "You know, I'm new in town, just here a few days. First time in Key West for me. It's nice to get to know someone who knows the ropes around here."

McMary, of course, knew that the Viscount had come out of the egg three days earlier. She heard about it the usual way in the Conch Republic, word-of-mouth, not from the newspaper. Like a lot of Key Westers, she didn't always read *The Key West Citizen*, the local rag whose best efforts are in its police log, where one can learn of the latest motor scooterist who slammed down on the pavement after one too many or a domestic battle between two locals who also had one too many.

McMary and The Viscount supped a few more cold ones, listening to an Englishman, trying desperately to play the guitar and sing, poorly, some Jimmy Buffet and Beach Boy tunes. Some people at the other end of the dark bar, near Greene Street, were giving the Englishman a bad time, and he was growing angry.

"Here, arseholes, you play the damned thing," he yelled, and damned if a woman in the group of four didn't walk over to his little bandstand and said she would. She played and sang, "Scotch and Soda," an old Kingston Trio song, and everyone agreed she was better than the Englishman. Even the lady bartender whose name is Kathy thought so. One got the impression that this was the only song the woman knew or knew well, so the Englishman took over once more. He wasn't bad, he was terrible, but then the daytime entertainment at Captain Tony's doesn't get paid much.

McMary asked The Viscount, "Have you been to the Half Shell? It's a great place for some steamers, if you like steamers."

"No, can't say I have," said The Viscount. "I'm getting hungry, though. How about you?"

"That's the whole idea. Let's go over to the Half Shell, have some steamers and conch fritters and some more beer. Very Key West, you know."

With that, The Viscount paid the bill for the two of them and walked out with McMary Marimba. He showed her how he mounted his nine-foot unicycle (he would set the thing almost parallel to the ground and run like hell and then jump on the seat, a technique that almost always worked). And she tagged along on her conventional bike, one of those with the bell and basket up front.

They were a strange sight as they headed down Greene Street and over to the wharf, down an alley featuring little huts selling silver and turquoise jewelry, cigars and bric-a-brac.

As The Viscount rode past the Schooner Wharf, another Key West landmark bar, some people jeered at him. A lot of crusty locals could be found there, and they didn't much cotton up to new arrivals. Naturally, The Viscount called attention to himself riding high over head. Gerald Jackwick, the venerable entertainer at the Schooner Wharf, looked around the stage and immediately started making up a song about the weirdos you see in this tired tourist town bar. His impromptu work was as good as his repertoire.

"Weirdos aplenty, weirdoes aplenty, where's this town going? Weirdos aplenty," he sang.

"I've seen it all from this wreck of a beer hall, and it's not gonna get better 'til we have our own kinda ball...and forget about the weirdos who are weirder than us all...

"Weirdos aplenty, weirdos aplenty, where are we heading? Weirdos aplenty.

"Can't put up with these out-of-town losers...no not these cruisers... not in our town of real doggone loafers...who don't need no more weirdos and cowboys from far-away places who just take our spaces...in our old beer hall.

"Weirdos aplenty, Weirdos aplenty. Where are we careening? Weirdos aplenty.

Some day we'll have enough and blow the damned place up...and they'll be no more tomorrows for the foreign weirdos who have no place here...and finally we can return to our bottles for a little peace and our kind of cheer...

"Weirdos aplenty, Weirdos aplenty..."

The Viscount rode by not knowing at all that the song was about him. McMary followed and she got the drift, but she liked this man who called himself The Viscount and didn't want to hurt his feelings, if that were possible.

They continued on to the Half Shell and got themselves seats at the bar and that was when they met Seamus Fine, salvager of lost treasures. What would happen after that would have a profound effect on The Viscount and on Key West in the days ahead.

CHAPTER TWO

Why Everything's Fine
With Seamus

The gentleman that McMary introduced The Viscount to at the Half Shell has quite a storied past. Growing up in the Williamsburg section of Brooklyn, New York, for some uncanny reason he developed a yen for the seafaring life. He thought it might have been due to a trip he took with Grandpa Fineberg into Manhattan in the early fifties. They took the subway over to the west side of the island and there Seamus discovered the incredible appeal of the great ocean ships that disembarked people and vast arrays of transported items from overseas. These ships to him were the grist of lore and mystery. 'Where did they come from, where are they going?' he wondered, as he sat there on the waterfront with his Grandpa, eating a knish.

Young Seamus grew into his teens and found that more and more he had to feed his fascination for the sea. When he was 18, he and his friend, Morky Golub, entered merchant marine school and found themselves quickly off to the lands of their imaginations. They had grown up together in Williamsburg, in the same apartment building just above an Hasidic hat store. That was a good thing because the owners sometimes would give them hat boxes and the two pals, as youngsters, would make sailing boats out of them and float them on a small pond a few blocks away.

Their first stop was with the Cunnard Line at Antwerp. From there they sailed to Amsterdam, the town that made them men, literally overnight. The older sailors took unmerciful glee in treating Seamus and Morky to a night out, a night of copious drinking, hashish smoking and the delights of the red light district. This was more than the pals had imagined. More of the same occurred in Oslo and Stockholm, though their trip to Helsinki put them off somewhat. They remarked that the people were so dour, so Finnish, not like the lively souls at the other ports.

Later, they triumphantly returned to the Port of New York and were transfixed by the Statue of Liberty, the harbor and the skyline, which they had never seen from that angle. Too, their parents and siblings were at the wharf when they arrived. They felt like soldiers of fortune back then in the early 60s. They had no worries, had plenty of pocket money, had smelled the sea and were pretty much foot loose and fancy free. They did not know that the Viet Nam War was just around the corner. These were good times, remembered for a lifetime.

Then the guys got drafted and weren't able to slide into the Navy, even though they had more than three years on the merchant fleet. They both wound up in the U.S. Army. Seamus became an information aide, and Morky a foot soldier. They both served two tours of duty in Nam and somehow both survived, amazingly so in that Seamus flew in helicopters constantly and Morky, who was with the Wolfhounds of the 25th Division, saw more human slaughter than any young man should endure.

When they got out, you guessed it, they returned to the sea and the Cunnard Line, which was waiting with open arms for these now veteran sailors to return.

Their travels took them to all corners of the world, moving rubber and timber from the Ivory Coast to Europe and the U.S., moving textiles and machinery from Argentina to Australia. Moving Volkswagen beetles from Bremerhaven to Baltimore and sometimes up the St. Lawrence Seaway to Toledo. There wasn't much they didn't see.

On leave one summer, when they were in their late twenties, the boys visited Key West for the first time. And they never left. They went to work for a treasure salvaging company, working on wrecks throughout the Caribbean. Some of these coins, jewels, gold bars, and artifacts were sold to dealers and other salvagers, such as Mel Simon in Key West, and even overseas. They originally worked for a small salvager who had a 35-foot diving cruiser. Eventually, they bought their own boat and opened their own business.

Two Jewish guys from the Williamsburg neighborhood of Brooklyn, New York, hunting treasures off Key West and becoming fixtures on the Key West scene. That's Key West for you.

❈

"Seamus, meet my new friend, The Viscount," said McMary cheerily. "The Viscount has just come to Key West, his first visit. I met him at Captain Tony's."

"Seamus, so good to have your acquaintance," said The Viscount in his formal way, adjusting his golden epaulets. If the people of Key West are as friendly as McMary, I know I'll have a good stay here – maybe a long stay, indeed."

"I've been here for over 25 years, and I never left except to go back to New York occasionally to visit family," said Seamus. "Traveled all over the world before that, with the merchant marines, settled here with a friend and that's been that. My friend, Morky, and I are both from Brooklyn, grew up near the Williamsburg Bridge, but we always liked the sea and here we are. Welcome to the Conch Republic. Even though I'm a Democrat at heart, I'm without a doubt a Conch Republican," Seamus snickered. "Where are you from, The Viscount?"

CHAPTER THREE

You Can Smell The Yeast On Greene Street

It is now four days later and down the way along the southern part of Greene Street, Costas Delupas is getting ready to open his Bulgarian bakery for the day. He calls it "Taste of Bulgaria" but it is really a combination of delicacies from exotic Grecian, Eastern Europe, and Isle of Man recipes. That's not the only thing he bakes. Shortly after the store opens at 9 a.m., Costas Delupas is fast on the phone taking bets from his clients from up and down the Keys. And he is known to sell some good dope there and even some of his own homemade vino. Well, actually it is like a Bulgarian grappa. Some people like it, others hate it.

Around 10 a.m. this day, the door chime rang and in walked a rangy man of about 6-4. He was in shorts and a tank top and he had a countenance on him that would piss you off. His name was Robert Cleverly. People took an immediate dislike to him and, in fact, he didn't much like himself as well.

Cleverly had moved down to Key West about six weeks ago, giving up his once thriving job in the advertising world in Chicago. Now, at age 47, Cleverly was trying to re-instate himself with a life. Trouble was he was the same son-of-a-bitch that he was previously, and he clearly didn't get Key West. The people at the Schooner Wharf and elsewhere among the true Key West bars could spot guys like Cleverly a hundred yards away. Guys like him walk with a swagger but make you really wonder why. Nobody in Key West could give a good damn about what Robert had done in his previous times. To them, he was just another putz. You can understand why Robert had to give up the world of modern advertising, for he had no real gifts; no, he hadn't come from the creative end; no, he was a senior vp on the account side of Hawkins/Flynn, one of the big shops in Chi-town. After a few years there, he blew out his welcome; it was his personality. He could do the work fine – if you consider that his primary job was to kiss the ample asses of corporate clients. Most anyone with not too much esteem could pull this off, and then treat the people back at the agency like shits.

The owners finally told him to take a hike. The creatives and media people had ganged up on him, as is their wont, and he could not survive. He had few friends, if you could call them that, had been married and divorced three times, and had no foothold on life. He sold his condo on Lake Shore Drive, took what was left of the earnings after the mortgage was paid off, some money he had in the bank and a gaggle of credit cards, and headed for Key West, though he had never been there before.

Sitting at the Schooner Wharf the other day, he got talking to one of the the regulars, a guy named Teddy, with a scraggily yellow grey beard, a guy kind of hunched over. Teddy was a bit of a panhandler and did odd jobs around the island. He usually had enough money to buy his beers and tequila. He kind of knew where things were around town. Robert, no never Bob, Rob, Bobby, always Robert had been watching this guy at the thatched roof bar for the past week, and figured he'd be a guy that would know something about the drug scene in town.

Robert, with his big gold Rolex on his left wrist grabbed the guy's right arm for a moment, as if Teddy were one of his long-lost friends, and perfunctorily asked him where he could get some dope. Teddy told him.

"Hey what's cookin', my friend? Name is Robert Cleverly and I was told to see you about some stuff…" Robert Cleverly entoned in a monotone as he swaggered into The Taste of Bulgaria. Coming from almost anyone else, Costas might have laughed at the question. Not this time. Not with this guy whom he had never seen before. Costas looked Cleverly up and down, and though Costas is only 5-5 to Cleverly's 6-4, he has broad shoulders and ham-like biceps and has the visage of an aide to Al Capone.

"Whatdya mean," rasped back Delupas. "This is a bakery – what 'dya think is cookin'? We have some nice raisin cake over there, just done. We have Bulgarian buttermilk poticia. Over there is lemon tarts from my Isle of Man recipe. You want some Greek bread, there you have it. What's cookin'? What's cookin'? You new in town?"

"Well, I've been here for a few weeks, just getting the lay of the land, if you will," said Robert Cleverly. "Somebody at the Schooner told me to come down here and he said to ask you what's cookin'," Cleverly added, winking oh so cleverly with his right eye through his horned rims. "The guy said you had the best stuff in town."

"What da hell you talkin' about?" lashed back Delupas. "Whad-ya here for, a pencil neck convention? What kind of bullshit ya spreadin' here? What ya see here is what ya get. Look it over, buy something, or don't buy something, and leave. No smart ass comments."

Costas Delupas has been overly sensitive this past year, and he didn't know what to make of Cleverly. For all he knew, Cleverly could be a Federal agent. This has not been a good year for Delupas, no, not since he got raided earlier in the year. Neither the Feds nor the Monroe County sheriff's department could prove anything, but nonetheless it was embarrassing to him, because people around town had made fun of him and what was worse, the daily rag, *The Key West Citizen*, had banner headlined a front page story,

"What's Cookin' At The Taste Of Bulgaria?"

Costas Delupas was a hard-working Greek immigrant who had been around town for the past 20 years; he had done all kinds of menial jobs until he had the money to open the bakery, which because he was a hustler, became so much to so many people. He had started running numbers before he opened the bakery, then after it opened, he moved into full-scale bookmaking, pot selling, even some hashish and coke. The bakery was a good and tasty front for all operations.

There was a deep throat within the sheriff's offices who had tipped Costas off to various potential intrusions – such as the latest raid – and with that notice, Costas was able to get all evidence out to a friend's houseboat, every last speck, the day before. Not having the material readily available, however, now had presented the problem of losing a good 3K a week in sales, and he was not happy. Baking stuff was hard work and long hours; his other business was a snap and much more profitable.

So Costas continued to look up at Cleverly and finally said, "Look, buddy, I can sell ya some cookies or some pear cake or maybe some schhstrudle with apples, or maybe I could just break you legs." On that note, Robert Cleverly turned on his heel and swaggered less out the door, buying nothing. He knew he had to find another contact for his dope.

.

As he walked out, McMary Marimba and The Viscount came into the store. "Hi, Costi, so good to see you my love, my honey," she greeted him.

He had a long-time crush on her. He was pushing 50, colliding through mid life and a widower. He always thought that maybe they would some time get together. Costas was surprised to look up and see The Viscount, a man who always was noticeably jolly. After dealing with Robert Cleverly moments before, he thought this was not going to be the best of days. Costas wanted to feel jealous as McMary introduced The Viscount as her new boyfriend, but The Viscount was so disarming and pleasant seeming that Costas could not do anything but give the man in the blue blazer with epaulets a warm welcome.

"I've been telling The Viscount about your delicious bakery," said McMary. "He said he likes crumble cake and I told him you make the best and I told him about your key lime pie, also the best."

"So good to make your acquaintance Mr. Delupas," said The Viscount, licking his chops as his nostrils inhaled the wonderful smells of the bakery. "This beautiful girl here is going to make me a very fat man when she's done with me."

Delupas looked across the counter and only hoped that he could be in The Viscount's shoes, shoes that today were black and white spectators. The cowboy boots were a little hot in the 90-degree sun, so he put them aside. Soon he would be wearing earth shoes. The Viscount always liked to keep his feet comfortable. That's where everything starts, he thought, from the feet on up. Today he was also wearing a Panama hat, to keep his head with the thick black and grey hair cool as well. Beneath his blazer, which was the one article of clothing he never was seen without, he wore a tee shirt with Captain Tony's sign emblazoned upon it.

McMary and The Viscount took their cake and pie and bade Costas Delupas adieu. As they left, Costas couldn't keep his eyes off McMary's upside-down heart-like ass. He wondered if The Viscount might not be too weird for her and he wished that it was he going out the door with her and The Viscount putting in a day at the hot bakery. He was maudlin but couldn't do a damned thing about it.

❄

CHAPTER FOUR

The Man Who Shoots
Paint Balls

JOHNNY GORDON LOOKED UP at the TV at Turtle Kraals and turned to a patron on the next stool. The man had asked him about the NFL football playoffs and wondered who he thought had the best teams.

"I don't care about any team sports," said Johnny, a 32-year-old machinist/fisherman from Mississippi who had been in Key West for the past two years. "I just like sports where you shoot things. I used to have a paint ball game room back home, where people would come and shoot the shit out of each other. I liked the game so much that I spent more time shootin' than I did taking care of customers. Ran that thing right into the ground. But I had this little 30-foot ketch and I decided to just take off from Gulfport and head to Key West.

"I anchor it off Christmas Tree Island and work a

lot of jobs over here in Key West. Got myself this little dinghy to get back and forth."

The gentleman on the barstool next to him just asked him one question about the playoffs and now he was getting Johnny's life story, not a very happy one.

"I catch a lot of the food I eat. Save a lot of money, and I'm thinking of moving to Costa Rica, where you can buy a house in the hills or even near the beach for a lot less than here. Goddamn, this is an expensive place. And by the way, most of the girls here are queer. I can't seem to find one who will live on the boat with me. You know, a girl that will help me out with the fishin' and cookin' and stay with me for some real good screwin'."

Turns out Johnny has an on again/off again girlfriend. Her name is Heidi Hamm, from Milwaukee. She's a flirt, according to Johnny, and goes off for weeks without contacting him. Some girlfriend, he thinks.

Heidi is only 5-2 but built like a brick shithouse. Strawberry blonde hair, blue eyes, beautiful white teeth framed by heart-shaped lips, high German cheekbones. Great butt, an all natural rack, and the shapely legs of a ballet dancer, but the whole package is shorter than your typical ballet dancer.

Heidi thinks Johnny is just a horny redneck, which he is. Heidi graduated from Marquette University and was captain of the field hockey team there. A lady jock. A tomboy through and through, but on top of that she was gorgeous. She'd come down from the north a few years ago after graduation to work on sailing boats. Parents have plenty of money and send it to her when she runs out of hers. Right now, she's just trying to have a good time, and why not? She's 26 and can snatch any guy she wants. Johnny, to her, is just a passing fancy. A real zero in every way. His lines of conversation are always the same – paintball, sex, shooting ducks, sex, catching fish, sex, and talking about going "big bear" hunting in the Dakotas. Grizzlies too, up in Alaska. She thinks he would really prefer to shoot his fellow man.

Heidi comes and goes, but Zero Belinsky can always be counted on. Zero helps him with the boat and with the fishing. Zero is pushing 60 and is a one-armed midget plumber, another Key West character. As with Johnny's work as a machinist, there is plenty of plumbing work for Zero. Zero likes to remind people that there is only one water pipeline leading from the mainland of the U.S. through the Florida keys.

"If that breaks, everyone will have hell to pay," he says in his squeaky but commanding voice. Zero maintains a pride in his work and thereby is much in demand by residents and commercial operations as well. Because of his 3-8 size, he has the ability to get into the nooks and crannies that a normal-sized plumber could never reach. He's strong too, with that one arm and has had the ability to beat much larger men in arm wrestling competitions, especially during Hemingway week in late July, when people from all over the country come to compete as Hemingway lookalikes. In fact, Zero himself looks like Hemingway, with his grayish beard. If Hemingway were alive, he wouldn't like this reduced resemblance of himself.

So Johnny can't find some steady nooky but he has one good friend who'd never let him down. Zero actually grew up in Key West, having been a Thalidomide baby with several birth defects, including being so small. In addition to being a midget and having only one arm, Zero was born with two stomachs, like a cow. With two stomachs, there was an actual benefit to Zero, for he could eat like a normal sized working man and did not have to go the bathroom as much as a typical midget whose own internal plumbing was miniature like his body.

But, more than anything else, Zero was a kind soul who somehow knew Johnny felt out of place in Key West, more out of place and self-conscience than most people would imagine. Zero's own problems helped de-magnify Johnny's. Zero made Johnny realize that all people feel out of place at times. He was a good role model for Johnny.

There was only one time when they have had a disagreement. Johnny had come back from a visit to the island in his dinghy and caught Zero schtumping Heidi in the galley of his boat, the boat which was 40 years old and had no name, no significance, somewhat like Johnny himself.

❈

Whitlow Wyatt was jet skiing with his new girlfriend, one he met at the Garden of Eden, which is on top of The Whistle, which is on top of The Bull, right on the corner of Caroline and Duval.

Whitlow had fallen in love with both Sea-Do-ing and his new squeeze, Pansy Riviera. Whit had come down from Buffalo for a week, his first time in Key West. He had come down with three other male friends – all four of the boys independent thinkers and doers. So they all went their own ways, getting together for drinks and sometimes dinner in the evening, wherever their spirits would take them.

Whit had never been on a jet ski, or Sea-Do as they call them, but he took to it well his second day in Key West. He went out with a group of six Ski-Doers and a guide. Took them about two and a half-hours to go around the full island. He did a header on his first trip, going about 60 miles an hour or better. Could have been killed. The crash was so harsh that he probably incurred a concussion. Whatever. But he was shaken up as he lost control of his jet ski and went right over the top, as the group was heading toward the famed Southern Most Point of the United States, just a hop, skip and a jump away from Cuba. When he got back on the jet ski, he noticed his Raymond Weil watch had been ripped from his wrist in the accident. His knees and elbows were all scraped up from hitting the shells on the shallow bottom of the Atlantic near the Atlantic Shores Hotel, more about which we will tell you later.

Whitlow was so enamored of the jet skiing,

however, he went back the next day and the next after that, at which point he made a discovery he had never expected... a body among the mangroves near the old slips the Navy once used for the storing of submarines that could immediately be called to duty if the U.S. coast were to be attacked by hostile forces.

When he wasn't skiing, Whit was looking for broads. On his third day in K.W., he found one, a willowy Eurasian who had grown up in Bakersfield, California, and was now living in Kato, Iowa. Her first time in Key West as well.

They met at the Garden of Eden, not a terribly well known establishment among the tourons but nonetheless a place that has its own quaintness. It is known for its body painting of women – and even some bold men, gay and otherwise. It is also a good place to drink and get some sun, and you don't have to wear your clothes while doing so. At night they have some pretty good local entertainment on stage and a whole phalanx of women who wish to have body parts painted. The place closes around 3 a.m.

Whit met Pansy during a hot Wednesday afternoon. He noticed Pansy sunning herself in the all together, and when she went up to the crusty little bar up there, he welled up the courage to get a conversation going. "How did you discover this place?" Whit asked her.

"I heard about it way back in Iowa, from some professors at the junior college in Kato. They told me almost anything goes at The Garden of Eden. And, ya know, I'm always looking for some kind of thrill, because things are pretty bland up there in Kato."

"How long have you lived in Iowa?" he asked.

"About five years. My boyfriend at the time and I were going cross-country on his motorcycle, on our way to Provincetown. I was only 19 and didn't know too much. Anyhow, I awoke at the motel in Kato and he was gone, never saw him again. I had about 20 bucks in my jeans and had to try to get a job to get enough money to get back to California, where I grew up after my family moved from Thailand when I was just a little kid.

"I got a job at the Friendly store back there, thinking I'd leave in a few weeks. Then I met another boyfriend and decided to take some courses at Wild Rose Community College, and I've been there ever since."

"Gee, that must be a lot different from where you grew up. Can't imagine a California girl staying in Iowa very long."

"Well, it's all about another failed romance and where that leads you or doesn't lead you," she said. "In my case, I went on to Iowa State, got a degree in education and ended up going back to Kato to teach at the junior college, while I was studying for a master's at I-S. Actually, I like Kato, not pretentious, not one Mercedes or BMW in the whole town. They all buy American there."

Pansy was ever garrulous, despite the fact that she was wearing no clothes. She invited Whit back to her lounge chair, where they talked through the afternoon. He wore a black thong but would not defile himself by taking that off.

❈

Just below The Garden of Eden, at the second-floor Whistle Bar, a thudding clamor presented itself to those seated on the balcony watching the passers-by on Duval Street, the main Old Town drag. 'Twas The Viscount arriving on his nine-foot-high unicycle. It was just high enough to allow him to land at balcony level, hop the railing and go inside for a beer.

The Viscount was becoming acclimated to Key West well into his second week on the island. Trailing just behind him on her conventional bike was McMary Marimba, her dark hair flowing in the breeze. She parked her bike and ran up the stairs, past The Bull, the bar on the street level, and met The Viscount at the bar above, The Whistle. They had become quite the cause celebre around town the last couple of weeks.

People liked The Viscount, though most were taken aback by his eccentricities. All the bar workers around K.W. knew McMary and liked her, too, so they accepted the Brazilian Admiral jacketed Viscount. He wore grey flannel shorts all the time now because the temperatures were always hovering around 90 during the day. He had a fine pair of Tony Lamas on his feet and now was wearing a sort-of white sailor hat on his head.

"Goooood day," The Viscount intoned to the day

bartender of The Whistle. "McMary would like a Pain Killer and I shall have a nice Killian's adjoined by a scrumptious side of Cuervo Gold, with salt, thank you." Georgie the bartender obliged. It was good to see McMary and The Viscount, 'cause things were slow this day at The Whistle.

The Viscount had decided to get off the Long Island Iced Teas he had been drinking earlier in the week. In fact, after having about 10 of those in one sitting a few days ago, he was laid down for more than 48 hours in the new pad he had acquired at Old Havana Lane. The lane is a short, short dead-end artery not far off the northeast corner of the Key West cemetery. He had remained in a prostrate position on his couch, with McMary coming by several times a day to feed him raw eggs, his hangover cure of choice, a remedy taught to him in his home country. Next to the couch was an old spittoon, in which he would spit out the eggs almost immediately upon their arrival in his stomach. McMary was happy to help, for she had never met a man so unsual as The Viscount. She thought a man with such a name would be haughty, but, of course, The Viscount was the opposite. She had never really wanted to settle down in her 20 years in Key West, but this time she found herself falling deeply in love with The Viscount, and he with her.

The Viscount mumbled something of his desire to take her back to his homeland with him after some time in Key West. But to this day, he never said where that home country was. In some cases, she wondered if it were even on this planet. She was Key West through and through and it would take a lot to move her away from the Caribbean charm of the old island.

Well, this was the first day of The Viscount's recovery, this day at The Whistle, and they both wanted to make the most of it. They walked over to the balcony to look down on Duval Street and the stream of cruise ship folks on a mission to buy tee-shirts and cheap trinkets to take back home with them. Everybody locked their bikes on Duval and elsewhere when they left them, even McMary, who locked hers to The Viscount's unicycle. The Viscount never locked his, not just because he was a trusting soul but also because it made sense to him. He could always order another from home if his were stolen. It didn't occur to him that the thief would be rather obvious and certainly caught before he left Key West or even got his way up the islands on Route 1.

In his homeland almost everyone rode a unicycle as a means of conveyance. The theory was this kept all souls in balance. Of course it had to, considering that even a two-foot high unicycle is hard to manage, let alone one that scales more than a story in height. Before the invention of the pneumatic tire, the people of his country used wooden wheels to get around for centuries.

Also in his country, people had given of themselves to help others. They listened carefully to the words of their shamans and yogis and most believed it important to be, as people, vessels of good to others. Consequently, there was much good perpetuated in his home land, and little evil. Just why The Viscount had decided to leave home was not known at this time, nor the reason for his landing at Mallory Square in the giant 20-foot egg, the construction of which his people had discovered centuries ago to be an amazingly agile and stable floating device. They reasoned that everything that wasn't a plant came from an egg, which in their native tongue meant safe encasement and avoided any comparisons to what happened to Humpty Dumpty.

As they swilled their drinks and looked out toward the melange on Duval Street, they saw Seamus Fine and Morky Golub walking toward Caroline. McMary yelled out to the two old chums and invited them up to join her and The Viscount.

The fifty-somethings galloped up the stairs to The Whistle, and did they have a story to tell McMary and The Viscount. They told the two an apparent murder had taken place in the old submarine slips, by the mangroves. They had just come from the Schooner Wharf and the story was ruminating around the outdoor bar. Not many murders take place in Key West in its modern, more civilized element, not like those that might have occurred in the twenties and thirties of Hemingway's *To Have And Have Not*, where the people had to be either rich or corrupt just to stay afloat.

"The Key West police and the Monroe County Sheriff's Department are all over this case; no identity; it must have happened in the past 24 hours!" Seamus hurriedly blurted out.

As Seamus and Morky talked about the murder, on the other far corner of the balcony sat Robert Cleverly. By himself. He seemed glum.

CHAPTER FIVE

Some Odd Behavior At The Atlantic Shores

THE ATLANTIC SHORES HOTEL is on the opposite end of the island, on the Atlantic Ocean. It is a deep blue and yellow establishment that caters mostly to gays and some gay blades – men and women – from Europe and, too, from around the U.S. It is really a motel with two long sections of rooms stretching from the street eastwardly to the pool and deck, including a pier that juts out into the ocean. This is another place where clothing is optional. Cameras are not allowed. If you were a painter, you would not be allowed either.

From about 11 a.m. until about 4 p.m. the place is usually packed when the sun is bright. Most people cluster in small groups or couples, not talking much to their neighbors, just taking in the sun.

At the head of the bar, a rectangle, there is what some refer to as the "Crow's Nest." There you can observe people to your left cavorting at the pool or look out onto the deck and pier and see others lounging in the sun. The Shores appeals to Key West's gay resident and tourist crowd, but there are plenty of heterosexuals there as well. Some in the altogether, like the gays, and others just ogling, carefully, from the nest, or from the bar or tables, to the right, next to a little short order grill.

Sometimes on Sundays they have a gay pageant that is rife with off-color jokes and cross-dressers strutting around better than most women do in the best beauty shows. Observationally, the women gays seem to keep to themselves and the male gays do so as well. In the background can be heard a P.A. announcement from the grill that "Gary and Arthur, your weiners are up." Giggles from around the bar. Always a joyous, festive occasion, especially for those clad in bathing suits or other attire.

This day Shallaha Obbst and Charla Severan, two lesbians, are sitting at the bar having some pinas, immersed in themselves. Sitting across from them are Gary Bluett and Artie Pepico, also gay and not at all familiar with the girls on the other side. Gary and Artie are not quite an item, just good gay friends. Sitting next to them is a hetero guy in his fifties, listening in as best he can to their conversation and watching toward the other side the overt romantic moves of Shallaha and Charla, who are in their own world. The older guy had just ordered a sandwich and decided to leave his friends in the Crow's Nest to sweat and bake in the sun. He was more interested in staying cool under the thatched roof, taking in the breeze from the Atlantic, than getting any more sun.

He overheard the two gay men talking in hushed tones about a murder that he assumed must just have occurred. The two gay guys were talking about going to a party that night – after hours – that would be "outrageous with info." The older man surveyed the bar assumedly thinking that there must be 12 or 13 others around it and there was very little cross conversation among them. Not unfriendly so much as it was narcissistic. The older man was a retired police detective from Philadelphia.

His name: Ted Obretta. He was thinking of moving down to Key West permanently, maybe doing some writing down there that would spin off his many years in the crime business. He was the oldest guy in the group of four men who had come from Philly and Buffalo. His best friend, Charlie York, a denizen of Main Line suburbia, was just 44 and was a buddy of Whitlow Wyatt, from Buffalo. York and Wyatt had known each other since their undergrad days at Brown University in Providence. York, a PR man who was the first product of his family over four generations to not be a doctor or attorney, had gotten to know Ted Obretta when York had been a police reporter for *The Philadelphia Inquirer*. Though there was about 12 or 13 years difference in their ages, the two had become friends a long time ago. The fourth guy, like Wyatt, was from Buffalo. His name is Zemblon Yurcocitch, and he practices podiatry in Niagara Falls, New York. He is the personal podiatrist of Whit Wyatt and a good buddy who shares Buffalo Bills season tickets with Wyatt, the scion of a family publishing business. Zemblon has always had a thing for feet; a placekicker at St. Lawrence University, he almost made it to the NFL but got cut by the Pittsburgh Steelers just before the regular season in 1979 and decided to head off to podiatry school.

The four made a hell of a fun group, three of them in their mid forties and the other a wise older brother figure who could not only keep up with them but could easily give them a run for their money most days. Only Zemblon was currently married. Whit and Charlie were divorced and Ted was widowed.

Ted walked over to the Crow's Nest and told the other three that he was going to have another drink at the bar and then head back to their condo in the Truman Annex, a place where northern snowbirds with money to burn liked to stay, a quiet place laden with vegetations and white picket fences, homes and townhouses. The four friends are old enough to know that sometimes it was wise to get away from the madding crowd of upper Duval Street and get some peace and quiet. They have been on many trips together, skiing in Beaver Creek or St. Moritz, or going on a golf trip to the Robert Trent Jones Trail deep in America's south, or a fishing journey to Costa Rica. They are good companions but also know when to get out of one another's hair. They all like hustling the chicks, but theirs is not the fraternity circuit or a gaggle of guys in their twenties who have no finesse or older guys trying to act young. They know how to pick 'em, when not to pick 'em and what is more hassle than it's worth.

Before Ted left The Atlantic Shores, he wanted to hear more of what Gary and Arthur were talking about, for he still had a sharp detective's ear and eye for things that were not quite right. He even looked over his sun glasses, watching the two lesbians from across the bar and a baldheaded sixtyish man sitting immediately to their right. He heard the bartender Shirley call out his name for another drink... the older guy's name was Dale. Ted wasn't working anymore but he just had this suspicion about Dale. Why was the guy sitting by himself, next to two lesbians eating each other's face? Why was he smoking unfiltered Camel cigarettes? Why did he peer downward to the bar, never looking up at the bartender as she gave him the beer? Why did Dale not make eye contact with anyone else at the bar?

Ted leaned over the bar and beckoned for Shirley to come over. He said, "Do you know that guy over there?"... as he looked at the guy's dirty finger nails and stringy long hair on the fringes of his head and watched him wipe his dripping nose with the back of his hand. "Yes, I do," remarked Shirley. "That guy is Shallaha's dad, Dale Obbst. He's visiting her and Charla from Cleveland. He's a painter, well, not a real painter. He paints cars at Maaco. Comes down every year this time. He puts up with a lot from those two. May I ask why you want to know about him?"

"Oh, nothing," said Ted Obretta. "I just thought he looked familiar."

So much for being suspicious, Ted thought. Maybe he had been out of the police action too long. The guy he was looking askance at was just a shy pig.

Meanwhile, Gary and Arthur were passing a notepaper with some handwriting on it back and forth. Over his shoulder Ted could see the words "roll" and "fat" at the top and a little lower down the page "kill… golden goose"…and then it was a word starting with a "p"…porcupine?…pirate?…pixy? What was the word, he thought. Then he resorted to an old police trick. He got up off his stool and pushed Artie to his right, almost knocking Artie off his own stool… feigned this being an accident…but still could not see the paper in full terms. Ted could now make out one of the missing words…it was, was…pel-, pel-… there it was, "pelican." He did not know what that meant but Ted Obretta, retired police detective from Philly, knew his instincts and he was back to work, even though this was his vacation.

❀

CHAPTER SIX

Be-Headed In The Mangroves

SHAMIR O'NEILL HEARD A thud under his 24-foot trawler as he was motoring just off the federally protected mangroves on the northwest side of the island. He thought it was a floating log that he had missed seeing as he headed back to the Gulf harbor. He had experienced this sensation many times fishing along the mangroves. His speed at the first thud probably wasn't even 15 knots, so he was unconcerned, and thought he'd jack the boat up to about 28 or 30 knots. That is when he heard a second thud at the back of the boat; and he slowed the boat down to almost a halt. Looking down Shamir noticed a dark substance, thinking the worst: he had blown his engine. He tried to speed it up again, and this time as he looked back a spray of liquid was shooting up in the air and toward him. He wiped some off his shirt, then realizing that this was not motor oil but blood.

Shamir O'Neill figured he had hit a manatee,

those large lumbering and lovable sea mammals that are on the endangered species list. They are on the list because they have become so domesticated after years of people feeding them fish and fresh water, as if they were in a zoo. The carnage wrought from powerful propeller blades is a true problem. The critters will even come right up to the boat basin on the Gulf side of Key West and wait for folks on the decks by the Schooner Wharf, Turtle Kraals and the Half Shell to feed them, even though there are signs every so many yards warning and pleading with humans not to do so, lest these sea cows become totally dependent on us.

The fisherman thought he must have hit the manatee while motoring slowly, then really coldcocked it with the rise in rpms as he sped away from the thickly set mangrove trees. His hope was that no one from the Coast Guard or local boat police would spot him. He thought the best bet was to get out of the mangrove area quickly and head home, leaving the carcass for other sea creatures to devour.

But Shamir O'Neill looked down again and realized that the form he saw below was too small to be a manatee. Whatever it was was bobbing beneath his vessel, near the propellor. As he reached down with his grappling hook to pull whatever it was from below, he discovered that the form was a human body, a chunky one at that – headless.

Shamir had been fishing Key West waters for nearly two decades and had never experienced anything quite like this. He began to panic, even though he could not be blamed for striking a floating body that must have been dead when he hit it and possibly decapitated it. People just don't go swimming in or around the mangroves. Still, irrationality got into his soul and he decided to relocate the evidence. He wanted no trouble with the law, not to even talk to the law. He had already been under their microscope for having allegedly done more than fishing from his boat.

Shamir was under surveillance for "possibly" assisting Cuban exiles in reaching the U.S. via his trawler, "The Blue Star." And, of course, there were allegations that he had been moving drugs from Cuba as well, much less illegal Cuban cigar products, to the keys and the mainland. The feds – the FBI and the Alcohol, Tobacco and Firearms people as well as the Coast Guard – could never get a hard enough handle on Shamir to bring him to trial. He figured he was conducting business on borrowed time and would avoid any encounters with his predators at all cost, though on their own account, they thought of him as a small-time Charlie. The Coast Guard and drug agents often find it a waste of time to try to knock off the little creeps. Controlling big time crime is their goal. Anyway, one guy with a small boat doesn't give them much thought.

Nonetheless, Shamir, slight of frame, not even 5-6, with a drawn long face, twitching black eyes and skin crackled from the KW sun, is usually nervous as all git-go because he assumes he is a criminal and people are watching him. He decided to dispose of the body and wash away the blood on the boat by turning back into the mangroves. He did so by setting the anchor out just a little below the water surface, throwing some rope underneath the arms of the beheaded and around the anchor and pulling them at slow speed into the mangroves. Shamir had no idea where the head was, thinking he might have snapped it off with his burst of speed after the first thud and hearing the second thud. No time to look for the head. Some of the clustering tarpon, barracudas and sharks might take care of that, he thought.

Shamir O'Neill got well into the mangrove trails, trails where small boats could negotiate; even Sea Doers were welcome as long as they cut their speed down to a few knots. His little 24-foot trawler was able to ferry around this surreal environment. He found an alcove and there he jumped out to pull the body off the anchor and deposit it between the branches of a couple of mangroves. The body probably never would be found, he thought, thinking like a criminal, although there was clearly no crime perpetuated by him on this hot late afternoon.

The next morning, a Thursday, Whitlow had Pansy on the back of his Sea-Do. They were taking themselves for a spin around the island without a guide or a small trail of fellow jet skiers. Whit had the confidence now to go anywhere he felt on the fast, little rental craft. Once out of the harbor, he took off as rapidly as the ski would allow him, showing off his dexterity to his new girlfriend from Kato, Iowa. They were probably going better than 60 mph, he was convinced. The jet ski livery guy at the pier in front of the Hilton figured Whitlow knew what he was doing on his fourth day out.

Whit especially wanted to go to the other extreme of speed and take Pansy through the mangroves, which she had read so much about. He thought that without the group jet skiers, he'd have a chance to do something romantic once inside the thickets that somehow anchor themselves to the Gulf's floor. He'd sneak inside one of the quiet and secluded alcoves and "do the deed" with his gorgeous, olive-skinned companion. She seemed up for it as well, or so he thought.

But first, Whitlow wanted to show Pansy the slips where the Navy used to hide their fleet of subs during the Second World War, the Korean War, and for quite a time later. This was the part of the trip that would be educational. He went about half way into one of the slips and discovered something that would change their day certainly – if not their vacation week. A body was brushing up against one of the mangroves that surround the old submarine slips. It had no head and it frightened them.

How could that body have transferred itself to the sub slip after Shamir O'Neill had carefully stashed it deep in the mangrove forest, in an inlet off one of the main boat trails? Well, being the fisherman he was Shamir should have known that strange things can happen when the tide goes back out, sometimes sucking objects a good couple of miles from their original position. In this case, the body – Mr. Headless – became dislodged from the forces of the ebbtide and went right back out the trail, out of the mangroves and into one of the slips, becoming lodged once more when the tide returned. O'Neill was not only not a good criminal, he was also an inveterate screwup.

"Geee God, Whit, what do you think happened here?" screamed Pansy, her yellow thong riding up her ample butt, her also ample chest crushing against her companion's back. "My, God, it has no head. Oh, God, no, no!"

"Geeeeez! I can't believe this. I can't believe this," rattled Whitlow. Three minutes ago he was thinking he'd be hunkered down with Pansy in the mangroves in just a bit, and now an obstacle he couldn't avoid was confronting him. He knew that if he just left the body and went into the mangroves with her, Pansy would think of him as callous and single-minded.

"Pansy, we must call the Coast Guard," Whitlow exclaimed in his most stentorian voice of command but all the while thinking, 'you dumb fuck, why did you have to show off and take her to the submarine slips first?'

For all he knew, the body probably wouldn't even be there when they came back with the Coast Guard. 'What a piece of crap this was.' He had always told himself that, with women, don't over do things. That usually had the opposite effect of that which you were seeking. 'I had to go the extra mile with her, showing her the submarine slips, and now we are going to spend the rest of the day screwing around with the Coast Guard. Jeezeeez H. Christ."

"Whit, you are so brave to handle this so well," Pansy told him as she hugged him.

Whitlow thought, 'maybe later, maybe later.'

Shamir O'Neill, the next early morning went fishing again, to do the things he usually had done. He thought to show his routine would be best if the drug agents or the police were observing him. Damned, if in passing the mangroves once more he didn't spot the head of the headless man he packed away yesterday. He thought if he were being observed, especially now that the body was found, he should turn in the head with the jolly big mustache.

The head looked familiar as he lifted it to his old wooden skiff. For it was. It was the head of Costas Delupas, the owner of Taste of Bulgaria and part-time drug dealer. Shamir put the head into a leather fish bag and took it to the Coast Guard station next to Conch Harbor. As he hoisted the head in the bag out of the boat to hand it to a Coast Guardsman, he noted to himself that it felt kind of light for a head, less he was sure than a bowling ball.

Shamir O'Neill was relieved to do this good deed… and he thought it would take any suspicion away from him. After all, he just innocently ran into the body while he was trying to fish. Nobody would draw any connection to him, he thought, since no one was around when he came across the body. Now he had turned in the head. A good deed. Maybe now he could return to his fishing, drug dealing, and Cuban exile transportation and get on with his horrible life.

❋

CHAPTER SEVEN

Bopping Around With Robert Cleverly

Robert Cleverly had a lilt in his walk as he padded down Simonton Street. Only in town three weeks now, he took pleasure in making acquaintances that didn't take pleasure in acquainting with him. A guy at B.O.'s Fish Wagon on Caroline Street told him about another great local spot, The Bottle Cap, way down Simonton, just a few blocks from the Atlantic. He walked into the Cap wearing a Tommy Bahama yellow-flowered shirt with a black background and beige shorts. Not Bottle Cap attire. He made heads turn as he entered the door of the little dive next to one of Key West's better liquor stores.

"I'll take a Bud Lite and a Cuervo Gold tequila on the side, salt and a lime," Cleverly jacked at the squat little bartender named Danny. Robert looked right through the bartender with unsympathetic, unfriendly eyes as he made the order.

Down the left side of the "U"-shaped bar, two biker guys looked up toward Cleverly, eyeing him with glances that would perturb most people. They didn't like the way he looked. Cleverly never noticed, as his putty faced emerged with a self-aggrandizing but subtle smirk, caused perhaps by being inwardly less than confident. Others at the bar noticed him as well because of his awkwardness but, in their doldrums in the late afternoon, just glanced him off.

But not the biker guys. No. They wanted to have some fun with Robert Cleverly. They moved down to the pool tables just behind him.

One of the guys racked up some six-ball and the other guy, a guy named Weasel, reared back on the break and hit Robert Cleverly right between the kidneys.

Danny the bartender had seen this show before and turned his back to the action. Others at the bar indirectly looked on in amusement.

Cleverly fell forward in sharp pain but didn't turn around.

"Sorry about that mister," Weasel muttered in the dark pub. "Not much room in here."

Next, Weasel, about five-nine and 225 pounds, stroked another backhand to the nape of Cleverly's neck, just as he had straightened up from the first blow.

This one knocked him off his bar stool and onto the floor.

"God, man, I'm sorry, there's just not enough room in this fuckin' goddamned joint," Weasel growled in some small appeasement to Robert.

As Robert writhed in pain on the dirty tile floor, between the pool table and the bar, Weasel dropped him another one. This time he hit him in the face with the handle of the pool cue, knocking off and breaking in two Cleverly's horned-rim Pierre Cardin glasses. Of course, blood just gushed from Cleverly's face as he sprawled out on the floor.

"Damn, I swear I didn't mean to do it!" roared Weasel, as the crowd roared back in laughter.

That was too much fun for the bartender, Danny, and he yelled to Weasel and the other guy and told them to "get the hell out of here or you'll be back at the County jail tonight, you turds." Danny wouldn't normally talk to such tough guys in this manner but he knew that they knew he was friends with half the sheriff's department and the Key West police, the latter not far down Simonton at Angela Street. And he knew they knew four squad cars would be on hand in two minutes if he dialed 911.

So Weasel and the other biker, a guy named Hreben, a very tall and thin guy compared to Weasel, dragged Robert out of the bar with them and gave him a few more welcoming blows outside. That was after

Robert, trying to stand up, fell against one of guys' black bikes and knocked it against the other one.

"What'dya trying to do to my bike? Asshole," shouted Weasel. Now outside, the two bikers decided to do "sport beat" on Robert some more. "You fuckin' snowbirds don't know how to act down here, do you?"

The six-five, 180-pound Hreben finally said something in a high-pitched, squeaky voice. "You asshole worm. You're going to pay for this."

For the next several minutes the two bikers proceeded to pummel Robert like he was a rag doll. And by the time they were done his smug visage had turned into something resembling an anchovy pizza.

Some bar patrons looked out the little window of the Bottle Cap and watched the bikers take off eastward toward South Street. Meanwhile, one of them called 911 on her cell phone and Cleverly was carted off to the nearby hospital on Stock Island.

Two of the guys at the bar were more concerned about the apparent murder of Costas Delupas. They held some compassion for the snowbird who just had his face shellacked but this wasn't the first time they had seen some transient bikers beat on a somewhat innocent but asking-for-it suit-kind of guy from the North.

Those two were Morky Golub and Seamus Fine,

the fifty-somethings who had grown up in the Williamsburg section of Brooklyn, New York and had been friends all their lives. The two guys who had now made their home in Key West for more than a quarter century. Morky had once been married but had been divorced now for a dozen years. He shared a house with Seamus, a conch bungalow on Elgin Lane. They had no gay proclivities. In fact, in their hey days they were quite the opposite but now, in their fifties, they had kind of resigned themselves to no longer chasing the skirts. In fact, they looked on with amusement as they watched younger men trying to make their conquests.

"Can you believe *The Key West Citizen* is two days behind this story?" Morky asked Seamus. That was not unusual in K.W., for word always traveled faster by mouth than by any other medium in paradise.

"Look, I never liked that guy Delupas that much, but you have to admit he was a hell of a baker. I loved his baklava," said Seamus.

"Yeah, and his marijuana cake was spectacular too," Morky countered. "Christ, that guy had more drugs in his back room than any friggin' place in Key West. But, compared to the big time guys in Miami, he was small enough a dealer that the cops and feds never paid him much notice."

"So you tell me why he was killed. Somebody must have been owed something by him and he wasn't coming up with the jismn."

"I don't know about that," said Morky. "He was a bit of a scoundrel; it could have been that someone just didn't like him and decided to waste him because he was buggin' 'em."

"How do you know it was a murder, even?" asked Seamus. "He might have been drunk, out there, maybe fishing or looking for a drug exchange, and just fallen out of that little crappy boat of his. Somebody could have run over him in the water, just like they do the manatees. Something like that."

"I'll bet you a hundred bucks right now that this is a murder. I'll bet you a C-note it is," Morky shot back.

❋

CHAPTER EIGHT

A Bad Night On Christmas Tree Island

JOHNNY GORDON HAD TAKEN his dinghy into the boat basin from his anchorage just off of Christmas Tree Island. He was going to stop by his favorite spot, Turtle Kraals and grab a couple burgers and have his usual four or five beers and head back to his ketch for the night. The sun had already gone down...it was maybe 7 o'clock. Johnny had had a long day working on a pipeline project on the northern side of the island. His friend Zero Belinsky had had even a worse day, having to crawl a good 100 feet into the four-foot pipeline to check for leaks. When he came out, not finding the leak after a couple of hours of searching with a headlamp on his yellow helmet, leaving the narrow pipeline, cursing, his whole body filled with a caking of brown-grey muck, he told the crew he had to puke. Not a nice sight for the crew...watching the 3-8, one-armed midget covered in God knows what, harking all over the place.

Zero steadied himself and Johnny felt sorry for him and told him to get a ride back to the ketch and they could hit the town after sundown. Have some fun. When Johnny got back to his boat, Zero said he was tired and sick from the day's work. He said he just wanted to rest on the boat. So Johnny went to Turtle Kraals on his own. Not so bad. He was a loner at heart.

So on he went. By now it was pushing on to 10 p.m. and he decided it was time to get in the dinghy and return to his boat, the boat with no name. He had another hard day ahead of him on a machining job. Time to hit the sack. He talked to no one while he was at Kraals, just ate his burgers with Swiss cheese, had a few fries and his beers and now he headed home.

As he gravitated back to the ketch, only a 10-minute jaunt from Key West Bight, the pleasure craft harbor, he had no thoughts. He just wanted to hit the sack.

Getting closer now to his boat, he noticed dark figures moving around in the stern section. And he got closer. At first he figured that Zero must have invited some buddy of his to join him for some beers. This did not please Johnny, who didn't want to deal with some guy he didn't know, visiting Zero on Johnny's boat, his beloved home at sea.

The closer Johnny got, the clearer the images became, silhouetted by the light of the moon.

Very soon later, Johnny discovered what to him was an atrocity. There at the stern of his boat, on the table where he often ate breakfast, were Zero Belinsky, his best friend, or so it seemed, and Johnny's erstwhile girlfriend, Heidi Hamm, going at it. Zero, the only guy Johnny trusted in all of Key West, was schtumping Heidi like a jackhammer.

Johnny's face turned crimson with anger. He was redneck mad, his carotid valves bulging.

Johnny started yelling and cursing at the infidels. He jumped from the dinghy onto his boat and grabbed Zero by his one arm and started to throw him overboard. This was not good because Zero, with only one arm, could not swim, and he could not walk as well, for the water was a four or five feet deeper than his height.

Heidi, young trollop that she is, started laughing, and, of course, Johnny thought she was laughing at him. She was and at the midget screaming that he couldn't swim. She liked to make Johnny jealous, and this one, she thought, really took the cake. What a bitch, though all would admit she was built like a brick shit house.

Then, suddenly, Johnny broke down. He broke down in tears and began trembling. What a rotten life he had. Even his beloved ketch with no name had been desecrated. What a rotten life.

Now even the little tart changed her mood. Zero felt joy, for now he felt he would not drown. Naked, Zero and Heidi cradled Johnny in their three arms, as he wept and the boat rocked back and forth from the wavelets created by the tide rolling in.

❋

Early the next morning, Zero awoke beneath a tree on Christmas Tree Island. He had taken the dinghy and left Johnny's boat. He thought it best to leave Heidi and Johnny to themselves, for Zero still thought of Johnny as a good, loyal friend. Zero felt remorse for schtumping Johnny's broad. He really did. And the guilt led him to the unoccupied island of Christmas trees. People really are not supposed to go on that island; it is there not to be commercialized. Something truly unusual in the K.W. area.

As Zero awoke, he noticed that his eyelashes and hair had become matted from the sap of the tree. He could barely open one eye and the other was closed shut completely. As he got up, he could just see the dinghy out there in the Gulf. He wanted to go back to Johnny's boat and offer his deep apologies for what had gone on the night before. He hoped his friend would forgive him.

When Zero reached Johnny's wooden ketch, all white and varnished from all of Johnny's hard work, he saw no sign of life. This was at daybreak and he knew Johnny would be getting ready to head to his job on Key West. There was no way for Johnny to get to K.W. without the dinghy.

Zero jumped on the boat and looked below decks. No sign of Johnny or Heidi. 'How could they have left in the middle of the night without the dinghy?' Zero wondered. He then noticed bloody handprints of two different sizes on the faux leather white seating cushions at the stern of the boat. There were other boats moored nearby in the Gulf surrounding Christmas Tree Island. Zero saw no one, for it was too early for most of these people to be up. If he could have swum, Zero might have looked in the seawater for Heidi and Johnny, but his guess was that they were taken away by someone intent on harm, while he slept soundly under the evergreen on the tiny protected island. Now he thought he should have stayed on Johnny's boat. He clearly thought he was at fault for causing all the malevolent troubles of the night before and the early morning.

His worst fear was that Johnny had killed Heidi and then himself; his next fear was that someone had taken them off the boat, for whatever purpose, and did them in. Perhaps a robbery. Johnny had been known around town to carry a bundle of cash in his right pants pocket. Also, Heidi wore a hideous amount of jewelry for a Key West inhabitant. Diamonds, pearls and sapphires, all hand-me downs from her wealthy German grandmother from Milwaukee. Johnny and Heidi would be an easy hit for someone determined to rob them. Zero knew that there were some modern-day pirates cruising the coasts of Florida, looking for opportunities. This had to be what happened, he thought.

Zero put in a call to the Key West Police. He felt smaller than his 3-8 frame, and he was deeply worried.

❈

CHAPTER NINE

An After-Hours Party Invitation

GARY BLUETT AND ARTHUR, or socially, Artie, Pepico were standing at the long bar at 801 Bourbon, in the heart of the gay emporia of Duval Street. They were holding hands, such is the custom on a happy night on the town. And there was more to come on this night of a private party, a shindig about which former Philly detective Ted Obretta would be more than curious. Before he had left the Atlantic Shores that afternoon, he heard the words "after-hours" party, which piqued his attention. He just thought in a vague way these guys had something suspicious about them. Of course to Ted, everyone had a certain suspicious nature until he knew them well. It was his custom.

By this time, Ted had heard definitive information about the reported murder of Costas Delupas in the mangroves, up northwest of the island. He hadn't been on a case in three years, but now his nostrils flared. He had just happened to have seen a little story in *The*

Citizen about the suspected murder, but possible accident, and decided he'd report some of his observations to the authorities. Ted would call the Key West Police and the Criminal Investigations Unit of the Monroe County Sheriff's Department, thinking that the murder in the mangroves might have implications beyond the immediate town. Monroe County covers all of the keys and more. Maybe this had something to do with drugs. He was sure the ATF was already involved, and probably the FBI and Coast Guard, so he decided not to call them. But Ted was the kind of detective who always thought about covering all the bases. Hell, in this case, on his vacation, he might just have a little fun and help out as well by supplying important details.

Ted decided he'd go out on the town by himself that night and check some things out. Since his quarry was the two gay guys he observed but didn't meet at the Atlantic Shores that afternoon, he thought he ought to go out looking for them, see whom they hung with. Watched what they did. He was in for a long night.

But before going out, he made that call to the Criminal Investigations Unit of the Sheriff's Department and on the other end of the line he got Deputy Lovie Jones, a veteran of hundreds of investigations in the keys, many of them drug-related.

"Yes," said Deputy Jones somewhat insincerely, "we can always use help in these cases, and I appreciate the fact that you're a former cop. We have a good-size staff but never large enough to go around in these types of cases. I've been in touch with the other offices around the keys to alert them of the case, and we've been working with the Key West police who are working with the Coast Guard in their jurisdiction.

"Why don't you come on by tomorrow morning after you do your checkpoints tonight? I'll be happy to see you."

Ted was accorded the respect one cop usually receives from another.

"I'll stop by your office in the a.m. and tell you anything I've come up with."

By the time Ted Obretta arrived at 801 Bourbon, a crowd had gathered. Some of them would drift back into the next room, which always had a lot more action going on.

A lot of non-gays visit 801 for a drink, a lot of couples. Everyone seems to get along there and the atmosphere is usually festive. Ted Obretta, still strapping and strong, fit right in there and he knew he could.

The former gumshoes had stopped by another predominantly gay bar, the Bourbon Street Pub, across the street, looking for his prey. He wasn't there long but did check out the place carefully, including visiting the garden bar and pool out back where he saw some heavy action going on, but no Gary and Artie. He was told by one of his bar mates that another good place to go was diagonally across the street, 801 Bourbon and the Saloon 1 behind it. "You'll meet some really dreamy people there," he was told.

Almost immediately, Ted spotted the two gays he had observed at the Atlantic Shores that afternoon. Ted was sporting a Panama hat with a black band. With this hat pulled down low, he could take wide peripheral glances at people without being obvious. He just wore a tee shirt with no markings, some cut-off jeans and deck shoes. He could have been a local, for all intents and purposes.

As Ted quaffed a Rolling Rock he watched the coming ins and going outs of the crowd in the back room. Some of the older gays were more colorful than the younger ones. They were dressed more gaily, not to make a pun, and they had more flair and self-confidence, gesticulating to one another, kissing and hugging. The younger ones were obviously hornier and – from Ted's point of view – almost sickeningly demonstrative. This did not make the overly hetero Ted cringe in any way; he had seen it all in his days as a detective with the Philadelphia Police Department. In fact, all this amused him. He had worked with all races and religions of people and even some of his fellow police officers were gay. He was not prejudiced. To him, someone breaking the law was the issue, not who they were or what their backgrounds were. He was a real pro in this regard. Perhaps, the most negative thing about Ted, though, was that he could not help but be suspicious, even when such thinking might not have been warranted. Still, he was a cop through and through.

Gary and Artie were not true lovers but they could easily get in the romantic mood, surrounded by many of their friends. Strange thing is that when people see two gays together they often assume that they are "a couple." Often not so. If Gary and Artie were out and about, they might kiss and hug, but more in a sporting way. Funny thing about 801 Bourbon, it was a comfortable place for most people. Everybody had a good, if not rowdy, time and gays and heteros mingled easily. Maybe the way any place should be.

By 10:30 or so, Ted was on his third Rolling Rock. He wanted to snap down a Cuervo Gold or two, but, to him, he was on an assignment and he did not want to become blurred. Besides, he wasn't packing heat. He had to have his wits about him, in case he got into some physical danger, as well. In his mid-fifties or even older, he could still take on most men in hand-to-hand combat. He was a solid 6-1 and a good 200 pounds.

Ted decided to take a peek at what was going on behind the Old West-style swinging doors in the back room. Some older gay men beckoned him in, and he nodded appropriately.

One of the men said, "Hey, big boy, this is the place where everyone plans for the after-hours parties. You might like to join one. That's when everything happens, after the real bars close around three or four.

You can't miss having a good time."

Ted smiled without saying a word. His intent was to case the back room and surreptitiously scan the crowd. He noticed that for the most part there were older gay men back there, a few younger ones in their twenties as well.

He saw quite a few characters in wildly colored kimonos and other assortments of costumes. And, then, he spotted a baldish older man, maybe pushing seventy, in a flowered shirt and pants. He figured the man had made his own clothing. These were not Tommy Bahamas or Polos.

The man's dress accentuated Kelly greens, bright yellows and oranges against a violet field. In other words, he stood out in the crowd. On his head was a huge fisherman's hat, the bill of which made him look like a… 'Pelican, that's it, Pelican,' Ted Obretta thought. And it couldn't have been a few seconds more that someone yelled out that name – "Pelican!" – and now Ted's ears were really perking. The guy was named Pelican; this must be The Pelican that the two younger gay men were referring to on their notepaper at the Atlantic Shores. Having a dramatic nickname was nothing new in the backroom. Many of the gays back there had a special name they called one another. As Ted observed the scene, he was sure in this instance The Pelican also had some station of nobility among the gays. He had seen enough for now.

Ted went back out to the main room for now and settled into his corner stool at 801 Bourbon. He continued to observe that room, eyeing the hetero couples, a few butch Lesbians and the younger gay guys, including the two named Gary and Arthur.

Suddenly, the bartender, a young kid named Meat, tapped Ted on the forearm. Meat said the guys at the opposite end of the bar would like to buy him a drink. Ted looked over to them and tipped his Panama hat in thanks. Shortly afterward one of them came over to say hello. It was Gary. He was just being friendly and not at all cognizant that Ted Obretta had been observing them that afternoon and night.

"Gary Bluett's my name, what's yours?" and he took out his hand to shake Ted's. "I saw you and your buddies at the Shores this afternoon. Nobody talks much to the foreigners around the bar. You probably didn't want to bother us and we didn't want to bother you. But, anyhow, I just wanted to say hi. You from out of town?"

Gary wore a black tank top, blue bathing shorts and flip-flops, and his partner, no shirt, red shorts and some ragged looking tennis shoes.

Ted, who wasn't the most engaging guy around, was kind of taken aback by this overt friendliness on Gary's part. "I'm Ted Obretta, from Philadelphia."

"Ted, we saw you sitting alone here and just thought we'd offer you a drink. How long you in town?"

"I'm here on vacation for a little more than a week. We, the four of us, take trips to different places from time to time."

"So where are your friends tonight?" asked Gary.

"Oh, we split up, too; we travel well together; just do our own thing and some things together," Ted replied, thinking how in hell did this gay guy get so much information from him so fast. This was Ted's suspicious and somewhat paranoid nature taking hold.

Gary waved Artie over to say hello to Ted. "This is my friend Arthur Pepico, Artie for short. We both welcome you to paradise!"

Ted shook Artie's little hand, almost as dainty a hand as that of a small woman's, and thought he'd make the most of this interaction with the two gay boys even though he was not one to pick up with strangers easily.

"So where you going tonight, Mr. Ted?" asked Artie. "You want to go clubbing with us?"

Not knowing what he wanted to do just yet, Ted said, "I don't think I'll be out very late tonight. We're staying at the Truman Annex, got a nice house there, and I think I'll just have another beer here and head back."

Artie, the more demure of the two gay guys, became a little more assertive and countered, "Don't do that. We've been invited to a grand party in the wee, wee hours. You should come with us. It will be the best!

It's at The Pelican's house on Mickens Lane. He's got a gor–geous house there. The Pelican is a big time insurance and financial services agent here."

Ted looked at Artie sympathetically and decided he'd give it a go, if only to draw in more information about this crowd. He especially was interested about the motivations of Gary Bluett; he thought little Artie was just a pawn for Gary and rather harmless.

And Ted wanted to know about The Pelican – a lot more.

"Well, if you don't mind an old man tagging along with you, I might take you guys up on this party. Just tell me where to go. But first I think I'll head back to the Annex and get some rest."

"You're no old man, Ted, you're a hunk if we ever saw one and we don't care if you're straight, we're just Key West ambassadors and want you see a part of K.W. you might not normally see," said Gary.

"We're off to see The Pelican… we're off to see The Pelican!" sang little Artie.

Ted finished his beer and headed down Duval Street, to Southard and on to the Truman Annex.

This was a party he wanted to be ready for.

❄

CHAPTER TEN

Blues In The Night

WHEN TED OBRETTA got to The Pelican's party on Mickens Lane, just off Angela Street, he was comforted by the fact that the Key West Police Station was not far away down Angela at Simonton. He had decided to walk down Simonton instead of Duval this late night, about 3 a.m., as there were still many revelers on Duval, too many drunks for Ted to endure. He had a nice gait to him, probably because in his mind he was on assignment, and he'd had a good two hours' nap.

Gary Bluett had told him to get to the Pelican's house between two and three in the morning, when the party would just be building. Gary told him it would probably go until eight or nine, certainly until after daybreak, as was the custom in these Key West after-hour parties.

The first persons Ted Obretta met as he entered The

Pelican's lavish Conch bungalow were McMary Marimba and The Viscount. He, of course, had never seen them before. He thought The Viscount was a bit odd, with his blue blazer and epaulets, the red poppy and grey flannel shorts, the cowboy boots. Maybe a bit affected, if not just odd. But 'hey, man,' he thought, 'this is Key West at it's wild and wooly best, so, so what?' And Ted thought McMary Marimba was a real looker. Ever the stern detective, Ted somehow thought he'd still find a way to enjoy himself this late night. He thought he had better, because this would be the best way to easily get the information he was seeking.

Ted was taken aback earlier when he walked down Mickens Lane. The first house on his left was dilapidated beyond belief, tilting in different directions. And there were some others down the lane that were in some lesser range of disarray as well. But as in the case of some other Key West neighborhoods in this south part of the island, standing with pride were a few other homes that had been artistically refurbished. One of these near the end of the lane was The Pelican's.

It was easy to find because even in the nascent stages of the party, laughter and some heavy-duty blues music could be heard wafting from the house.

The scene was already crowded when Ted got there. A number of the people were gays, both men and women. Some were hanging on one another amorously and others just trading stories. Like Ted, some were quite obviously attending on their own. Ted made a quick scan of the bungalow and saw no signs of The Pelican or Gary and Artie. He decided he'd move through the crowd ever so slowly, taking up idle conversation and at the same time picking up info that would give him some fix on the Costas Delupas murder. Ted clearly assumed that it was a murder and not an accident, as the local newspaper was conjecturing. It is not good for anybody's business to have a murder in paradise. Ted went back to work.

"I just love these Key West parties!" said The Viscount. "Everyone around here is as friendly as can be."

"Ted Obretta is my name. I'm from Philadelphia. Just in town for a week or so."

"This lovely lady is my gal pal, McMary Marimba. She's been a Key Wester for a couple of decades."

" Pleasure to meet you, McMary. You have quite an unusual name there."

"Oh, it's my father's idea; he's a real jokester. He's Mexican and my mother is Scottish. He didn't want to cheat my mother's ancestry, so, instead of a typical Mexican first name, like Consuela or Teresita, he made up a name that sounded Scottish. So there you have it." McMary's black eyelashes fluttered and her jet-black hair nicely set off her plunging white halter-top and her yellow short shorts.

"And where might you be from?" asked Ted of The Viscount. "You seem to have a bit of an accent, a bit of British."

"Oh, I'm from quite far away," said The Viscount. "But for now and perhaps forever I am a Key Wester."

"I'm curious. Do you know the people who are throwing this party? I sort of fell into this thing at the last minute, just tonight," said Obretta.

McMary responded, "I've been living here past 20 years and that's the way these things usually happen. Someone thinks up a party the day it is to happen. Word spreads, and voila, you have a big party. Usually you know someone who is spreading the word who has been given the word by someone else. There could be a hundred people, fifty people, or just a small group. It stops when the last person stops spreading the word.

"How did you hear about it, Ted?"

"Well, I met these guys, Gary and Artie, over there and they just invited me a few hours ago." Ted pointed across the room, into an alcove where the two were standing and now waving at him and beginning to work their way through the crowd to greet him.

"I'm old enough where I had to take a nap after 10 o'clock to be able to make it here at 3 a.m."

"Have you met The Pelican?" asked McMary Marimba.

"No. But I believe I saw him at the back room at 801 Bourbon... I think it's called Saloon 1, or something like that.

"You know I have to say I like the way other people invite newcomers to someone else's party in Key West," Ted continued. "That usually doesn't happen very much where I come from. It's more formal, with printed invitations and a very specific mailing list. Up north we may be a little worried about a random party like this."

"Well, this is Key West and everything and everybody just hangs out. It's very convivial down here," said McMary, with The Viscount smiling affectionately down at her.

"I'm looking forward to meeting the guy who owns this home. He must be a generous man to his friends and acquaintances," Ted responded.

"Oh, you will, you will," responded McMary. "He makes his point of making the rounds and especially meeting the new people."

"What happens at these parties? What goes on here?" asked Ted, almost wishing he hadn't come out with those phrases, thinking he was acting suddenly like a detective and not just a party goer. 'I've got to watch myself or I'm going to be a little too rigid and abrupt and they'll start to clam up.'

McMary said that everything is kind of spontaneous. "People who come together usually stay together, singles try to meet other singles if they want. Groups of several either stay that way or leave when they want. Some who hear of other parties in town might go catch them as well. And, if you stay long enough, you'll see a whole stream of people coming and going."

Ted wanted to ask her if the party people do drugs, have sordid sex, pass on rumors that should be checked out, jump in small piles... He wanted to ask those sorts of things but, if so, he knew he would seem too uptight, like an interrogator. If he did so, he knew he wouldn't get what he was looking for, and he had to admit he wasn't sure exactly what he wanted to know other than to get more info on the Delupas murder. He thought people at the party might have some answers.

He didn't know what to make of the man called The Viscount. He thought it odd that The Viscount seemed to let McMary do all the talking; maybe The Viscount was smart enough to let McMary do most of the talking to a stranger, especially about Key West traditions.

By now Gary Bluett and Artie Pepico joined the group and gave Ted high fives of welcoming. It was the garrulous Bluett that Ted thought might feed him the kind of information he was seeking. Artie seemed too out of it and goofy to be of much help.

He thought it interesting that Gary and Artie seemed to know The Viscount so well, a fellow, for all intents and purposes, who was a new man in town, just like himself. The two gay friends kissed everyone in the European manner and gave McMary a big squeeze as well. She, Ted thought, seemed to look at the two almost seductively, surmising, in his own suspicious way, that straight women always seemed to be wanting to convert gay men to the hetero lifestyle.

It was just then that the colorful older man, The Pelican, ambled up to the group.

"Welcome! Welcome! Welcome!" said The Pelican, almost shrieking with joy.

"Please enjoy the wonderment of the lovely people here tonight," he continued. "They are a combination of what Key West is all about." The Pelican knew everybody standing next to him, with the exception of Ted Obretta, whose back he rubbed affectionately.

"So good to have you with us Ted. I saw you at Saloon 1 earlier, and I am so happy that Gary and Artie invited you to this big party tonight. Aren't they delightful folks, Ted?"

"My pleasure to be here. I didn't expect to get invited to an in party like this. Just here on vacation, you know."

"Well, Ted, everyone calls me The Pelican, but my real name is Ramsey Fletcher. I'm in the insurance business. Key West has been good to me the past 30 years and I just like to share whatever I have with my friends. Just have a lot of fun here, stay as long as you like, stay all night and the next day, too, if you'd like."

Ted thought Ramsey Fletcher, The Pelican, was coming on to him and that could be so. But then Ted thought maybe the guy is just demonstrative, arms flailing lovingly and baldish head with white pigtail bending backward for emphasis. The Pelican's ice blue eyes betrayed another, almost evil, nature, Ted thought, and he had better learn more about what this meant.

"Move through the crowd. Move through the crowd! Teddy," The Pelican entreated. "Meet these delicious people! They're the best, the very best!" And that's exactly what the ex-detective from Philadelphia was about to do.

Finally, The Viscount chimed in. "Hey, Ted, let's do it together with McMary. I want to get to know some of these people too."

Ted, thought, he sure as hell could operate better by himself, wending his way through the crowd at The Pelican's. He had the idea that once The Viscount got started he'd be a real magpie and that might wreck Ted's m.o. But there was a bonus if he looked at the other side of the coin.

The good side to this was that McMary was obviously a real good social connector and would help the process along for Ted. Men and women – straight and gay – probably liked her because of her natural wiles. Maybe she'll keep a lid on the character she's with, just like she seemed to have done with Ted.

Ted thought not only did The Pelican have good

taste in decorating, he also had a smart affinity for the right music. He had some light blues music played live by an old black guitar man, in the background. People could hear themselves talk, but the old black man set a nice background tone.

McMary, The Viscount and Ted started talking some more with Gary and Artie.

To Ted's dismay one of the first things Gary said was that his buddy Artie had made some "really scrumptious egg rolls and Lebanese fatoyer" for the party. "We should try some!" Gary beckoned to a table of colorful assortments of food aromatically wafting toward them from a large serving table. In the middle of that table, Ted noted, was a golden goose ceramic, out of which the partygoers were ladling a heavily spiked punch.

Ted thought back to his suspicions about the notepaper that he had tried to observe the previous afternoon at the Atlantic Shores bar, and he realized that once again, as he was wont to do, he had jumped to conclusions. What he had been reading, no doubt now, was Gary and Artie's list of things to bring to The Pelican's party. Probably, he thought, their reference on paper to "the golden goose" was about The Pelican and his ever-present party symbol – the golden goose serving bowl. And Ted had been wary about this earlier, as perhaps an indication of misdeeds connected to the murder of Costas Delupas. He could have kicked himself.

CHAPTER ELEVEN

**What Shallaha & Charla
Heard At Pearl's Patio**

TED OBRETTA MOVED through the crowd at The Pelican's, disappointed that he had over-stated what he thought were leads in the Costas Delupas murder case, trying to catch other word about the murder, word that should be rampant at a party like this. And it was.

By now, he must have met a good dozen people and at this point he found himself, McMary and The Viscount talking with the lesbians he had observed at the Atlantic Shores the day before. He got the distinct idea that many of the people at Ramsey Fletcher's (aka The Pelican) party were denizens of the Atlantic Shores, a place on the Atlantic that catered to gays, nudists, straights, Europeans and all four, among others. He had been to the Atlantic Shores on South Street near the east end of Duval on two occasions this vacation week and now, as he glanced through the crowd at the party, he met or observed more than a handful of folks he had seen at the Shores.

Shallaha Obbst and Charla Severan were holding hands as they spoke with Ted, remembering him from the Shores. When they now found out that he was an ex-detective they quickly switched the conversation to the be-heading up in the mangroves of Costas Delupas. Ted could have killed The Viscount for divulging this, for Ted preferred to work this detail incognito, just another middle-aged guy from Philadelphia was he. That's the way he wanted it but his new magpie friend couldn't resist spouting off. The girls felt comfortable with Ted, however, especially in the presence of McMary Marimba, whom they adored, and not for sexual reasons. A lot of people on the island new McMary and those people liked her for being the natural, good humored soul that she was. They were somewhat incredulous with The Viscount, however, and that was because they both thought he was "over the top, let's make fun of Key West" in his clothing and demeanor. Charla had spotted him from across the living room and had pointed him out to Shallaha as appearing to be quite the ass. But, unfortunately, this was just the way he was – naturally.

Then it wasn't long before the girls were gasbagging with Ted about the murder. They had their suspicions.

They told Ted about this guy who had arrived in town from Chicago, an ex-advertising guy named Cleverly. That he had been beaten to a pulp by some unnamed bikers just outside the Bottle Cap bar that was a favorite of locals. They thought the two acts of violence – the murder of Costas Delupas and the beating of Cleverly – were somehow connected. Ted was listening attentively at this point.

Shallaha told him about a conversation they had overheard at Pearl's Patio, a bar within Pearl's motel, a place catering to the lesbian crowd.

"Somehow, I think the guys who beat up Cleverly had picked him out of a crowd and decided that they had to scare him out of town. Some of those kinds of guys rely on the drugs. Delupas was a provider, even though the police could never nail him on those charges," she averred. "I think they were pissed, those bikers, because they think Cleverly had something to do with Costas's death. One of the girls at Pearl's had told the bartender that Costas was really honked off about this Cleverly guy who was putting on airs and trying to get into the bakery shop's backroom operations. Of course, one reason Costas never got caught by the police is that he would never, ever, deal with strangers. And here comes this guy busting in on him like the guy was doing a deal in Chicago or New York. No way, Jose."

Ted said, "So why do you think the Cleverly guy would be implicated in the murder? I might guess it would be the other way around. The baker might have taken out his wrath on Cleverly."

"No way," exclaimed Shallaha. "Costas Delupas

had a big, big growl but even though he was doing some dirty deeds, he wouldn't hurt a flea. He was a Greek – a lover, sex monger, a roly-poly jerk but never a murderer. And, by the way, mister detective, he was the one killed, not the other way around."

Ted was taken aback at Shallaha's brazenness with him but he was careful to not act defensive. He didn't want her to know he was working the case; he'd prefer that he be considered just a visitor who happened to have been a detective. It might be thought, as well, that Lovie Jones, the deputy in charge of the case in the Monroe County Sheriff's Department would not be simpatico. What with the Key West cops, the state police, the FBI, the Coast Guard, the Navy military and God knows who else traipsing over themselves on this case, Lovie truly did not look forward to an ex cop coming off the bench and getting in the way.

"Well, are you suggesting that Cleverly out-and-out murdered Delupas, or what?" asked Ted Obretta with a tinge of sarcasm intoning his voice.

"Well, sir, I don't know what to think. I'm just imparting info," Shallaha shot back.

All this while The Viscount listened intensively. Where he hails from there is no crime, no laws, no detectives, no judges… it is a place of peace and good deed to fellow man. But more about that later.

Meanwhile, Ted thought that maybe he should pay Robert Cleverly a visit. Where would he find him?

Being a detective, the first place Ted would look was in the hospital, where he thought Cleverly most assuredly would be, based on the description of the beating he had remembered seeing in *The Key West Citizen,* and from what Shallaha had said.

CHAPTER TWELVE

Why A Boy Goes Wrong

THE FBI TURNED UP some inviting evidence this day, some three weeks after Costas Delupas was found decapitated, murdered in the mangroves.

Upon investigation of the various suspects in the crime they noted that Robert Cleverly had had an aka. The name was Stephen Speciel (pronounced Spe-cheel), a man who had hailed from Grevey, Idaho, a nice little ranching hamlet smack in the middle of that state.

You have to turn back the clock to get a full understanding of Steph, as he was called back in his days as a youngster and a teenager.

Mr Heimetz, his teacher in the fifth grade at the Argonne Elementary School, had been very harsh one day on the lad. You see Mr. Heimetz, who was not having a very good time at that time with Mrs. Heimetz, took out his wrath on the sensitive youth, accusing him of ripping off an essay from *Boy's Life*. This was back in the late 1950s. For some reason Mr. Heimetz was an avid reader of *Boy's Life*, had been when he too was a kid.

This story was about a Shoshone Indian boy who had captured a loon frozen to the rocks of a brook in the dead of winter. The boy took a sharp edge of an arrowhead and chipped the bird free, took it home to his teepee and kept it warm under the covers of a beautiful puce, lemon yellow and black blanket that his grandmother had woven many years earlier. When the loon and the boy woke up the next day, the loon bit the boy on the index finger. This scared the young Indian boy and he let the bird go, the bird fed, rested and happy. Now the bird sought no further aid and wanted to return to his flock. Well, so much for that story.

The problem was, however, that Mr. Heimetz had seen that exact story line in an old *Boy's Life*, one from back in the early 40s. He had all the editions, and he had checked his memory out and confirmed his suspicions. There were few material changes in the story line in this act of conscription by Steph, Mr. Heimetz thought, and the next day Heimetz let him have it. Trouble was the whole thing was a coincidence. Stephen Speciel had made up the story of the Shoshone boy and the loon. He had never seen the old copy of *Boy's Life* and that was that, except that this left a permanent scar on Steph.

Mr. Heimetz was still in the classroom when Stephen ran out crying and, frankly, Mr. Heimetz took stock of what he had accused the boy of. Mr. Heimetz had second thoughts about this seeming plagiary and he rushed after the boy, but couldn't find him. Steph had loved to create ideas about the Indians and nature and he often would put his thoughts on paper. Though he was not particularly a good student in English studies, when he was interested in a topic, things seemed to flow naturally. Mr. Heimetz had jumped to conclusions because he thought the boy wasn't his best student in English. He had trouble with diagrams and wasn't that good, Mr. Heimetz thought, with his essays.

But now Mr. Heimetz thought what if the kid had actually made up this work himself? How would the kid have ever found a copy of *Boy's Life* of that early 1940s vintage anyhow? The Argonne School library didn't have them but one year back, and the downtown library in Grevey had them back only a decade.

Since Mr. Heimetz couldn't find the crying boy as he searched through the school and outside, he went home and took it out on Mrs. Heimetz, who was then home cooking the family dinner – squab and beans. This was one of the reasons the Heimetzes had a bad relationship. They were always taking things out on each other, not being sympathetic to the other's problems. Today we know this as the primary reason marriages go bad, but back then in the late 50s when everyone but Hollywood stars stayed married, no matter what the problem or agony, normal people stayed together – and took out their wrath on young innocents such as Stephen Speciel.

Stephen had run home that afternoon crying and whimpering. It was yet another in a series of setbacks in the young man's life that would cause him to be the antisocial and insincere prick he is today.

You might think this overstatement but not I. There are many examples of the discordant life that Stephen Speciel from Grevey, Idaho, had to endure and later perpetrate. He became more and more aloof as he went through his teen years, preferring to riding his horse, named Jack, doing poorly in all courses at the Admiral Grevey Senior High School, staying away from the girls, and having pimples. It was a horrid life.

Like his adult predecessors, Stephen started taking out his ill feelings against others when the opportunity presented itself.

He was asked to leave Grevey permanently in the late 1960s after he was accused and convicted of being the serial murderer of 14 prize hogs at the Ramadam Ranch in the small town of Gesper, not far from Grevey. Over the course of two years the hogs were slaughtered. The sheriff and his deputies could not find the culprit, nor any evidence of the culprit's modus operandi. All the hogs were decapitated or worse.

But one day Stephen Speciel got caught up in his own tracks and a vigilante group of townsmen apprehended him just as he was about to slice into another prize hog. In the old days he would have been hanged, but in these times he was put in the county jail for six months, the same amount of time one would serve for possessing marijuana. But there was one other piece to this penalty. Steph Speciel, now age 21, was forced to leave his home town and never set foot it in it again, nor in Gesper, where he had committed these heinous crimes. He was lucky to get out before a member of the Ramadam family blew his brains out.

From there, Stephen Speciel left his home state for Chicago, where he became an advertising man and took on the name Robert Cleverly.

CHAPTER THIRTEEN

A Visit To The Hospital

TED OBRETTA PAID A visit to room 316 at the Lower Keys Health System's hospital on Stock Island. The guy in the room had been in intensive care for the several days before being transferred to a regular room. He was beat up pretty badly.

This was the day after Obretta talked with Shalla Obbst at The Pelican's party.

Ted had not reported yet to Sheriff's Deputy Lovie Jones any of the latest in his discoveries. If Jones knew that, it would be just as fine with him. But Ted couldn't help himself. Gumshoes that he is he had to keep his nose in this investigation even though he should just plain be on vacation. But this work, to him, was better than lying around in the sun or getting soused in the Key West bars. No, he was mounting his own case and would deliver the goods to Jones in due course.

When he looked into the room that Robert Cleverly occupied even Ted was horrified at the sight.

One eye was sticking out, as if it were on a slinky spring. The other was patched. Both arms were in casts. And the dome of his head resembled a blue sapphire bowling ball. One ear was also bandaged. His jaw was wired shut, apparently, and he made hissing noises when people approached him.

Ted knew it would be hard to communicate with Robert Cleverly, but being a guy who seldom knew the word quit, ex-detective Ted Obretta was going to try his best to get information.

Robert, who was alert considering what he had been through, would be able to hiss his answers, if he would work with Ted, who explained his involvement in the case as that of being an interested bystander. One hiss was yes, two was no. Three hisses would be, "I don't know offhand." Four hisses would be, "I don't agree with your question and do not wish to answer."

Here is how it went:

"Do you know the people who beat you up?"

"Hiss... Hiss... Hiss!"

"Were you involved in any way in the disappearance and ultimate murder of Costas Delupas?"

"Hiss... Hiss... Hiss... Hiss!"

"Seems to me you are avoiding my question," said Ted Obretta. "How about a simple yes or no?"

"Hiss... Hiss... Hiss... Hiss!" This was probably Cleverly's way of taking "the fifth."

"OK, would you have killed Delupas if you had had the opportunity?"

"Hissssss!!"

"Did he try to kill you?"

"Hiss... Hiss!!"

"Were those guys who beat you up connected to Delupas?" asked Ted.

"Hiss... Hiss... Hiss... Hiss... Hiss!!!!"

"That's five hisses... what does that mean ? Maybe?"

"Hiss!!"

"Look, I know you are under the weather but I want cooperation here. You could be in serious trouble when you get out of hospital. Those bikers could come back and get you and the next time it won't turn out so well."

"Hiss... Hissssssss!!!!!!!"

"I take that to mean , 'No.' Is that right?"

"Hiss."

"Look, buddy, I don't know if you are the troublemaker in the Costas Delupas case or if you are the simple victim of random biker abuse," barked ex-detective Ted Obretta.

With that, Robert Cleverly passed out and moments later the floor nurse asked Obretta to leave.

He knew not whether he had picked up valid information or not, but he would report what he had found out to Sheriff's Deputy Lovie Jones as soon as he got back to the main island.

Jones was in no mood for more invasion of his turf by Ted Obretta. He had another problem that was concerning him, the disappearance and possible homicides of Johnny Gordon and Heidi Hamm from the day before.

When he told this to Obretta, Obretta said that he was convinced that the beating of Cleverly, the murder of Costas Delupas and the mystery of Johnny Gordon and Heidi Hamm were all connected. "Trust me, buddy, it all makes sense."

"My God, man, have you lost all your marbles?" rebuked Deputy Jones. "You are, get this, on vacation, and suddenly you have become the Columbo of Key West. I appreciate your interest, man, but don't go telling your thoughts to any of the other law enforcement agencies, like the FBI and the firearms and drug agents. I'm enough. And, by the way, we have already arrested a suspect in the Gordon/Hamm case. He is Johnny Gordon's friend, Zero Belinsky. Belinsky is also being interrogated for possible connections in the Delupas case."

"Who is this Belinsky guy?" asked Obretta, not being able to keep his nose out of where it shouldn't be.

"He's a local character, a midget plumber with one arm. Looks like Hemingway."

❋

CHAPTER FOURTEEN

The Viscount Gets Serious

IN TWO WEEKS TIME The Viscount has gone from splendor to squalor. But no matter. He is in love.

The Viscount has found himself running out of pesinos, the currency of his native land. But he shall call for more. They shall arrive in the next egg landing at Key West but he isn't sure just when that will be.

Yes, he has gone from the cottage at The Gardens, one of the most exclusive places in Key West to the ramshackle manse on Duval and United that appears to have been the model for the house the Munsters lived in. This is the sprawling house that, on the southwest corner of Duval and United St, has shutters flying every which way and has not seen a coat of paint in maybe forty years.

It is big, however. And many strange people have lived in it, giving the weird and jaunty The Viscount, by comparison, an air of aristocracy, which should be so in any event because of his natural demeanor.

Thinking back the last couple of weeks, The Viscount is somewhat concerned that the pesinos have not arrived. He liked staying in the cottage at The Gardens, a beautiful and bountiful botanical feast of foliage and 17 fine rooms and the one cottage. Key West has more beds and breakfasts per square centimeter than any place on earth and The Gardens is among the finest of them. But he reckoned that, what the hell, he had been at the cottage for two weeks and his beautiful squeeze McMary had been with him. 'Shan't get better than that,' he reckoned. And, oh, is he in love.

But now he has gone from the sumptuous quarters of The Gardens to the munsteresque wonderment of the no-name but large house on Duval at United. He is hoping that the next egg will arrive soon, hoping as well that his mother shan't be in it, not that he doesn't like his mother but more so that he doesn't want to accede his attention away from McMary Marimba. As he rolls over on his skanky mattress on the floor, with the love of his life next to him, he ponders how long the remaining pesinos will last. He would like to bring McMary back to the wonderful life he has been accustomed to.

"The Viscount, honey, why do you use an egg for transportation?" asked McMary. "We have been in love for two weeks now, a long time in Key West, and you, my love, have never told me why you come in an egg."

"It is a long story of my land and my people's purpose, but let me say that in my land, which is something I should tell you about now that we have become so close, we have a special sense of aerodynamics. First, our eggs float and they bob with the wind and the many roils of the sea. The shells cannot be penetrated from the outside, just the inside, at the time that we wish to exit.

"On the Isle of Goda, specifically at the Slippery Eel Yacht Club there, I learned to egg sail. This is quite a sport, McMary. The sailor is implanted in an egg – in various sizes, depending on his or her age, size and body type. It is cool inside the egg and the feeling in there is quite miraculous. We learn to race these eggs on Sundays and if you win the championship in your category you are granted a new egg and some 10,000 pesinos to spend on whatever your heart desires. Later, when you become quite adept, you sail these eggs to distant places and return to a hero's welcome at the yacht club. Unless something goes wrong. I had always wanted this to become an Olympic sport, but, you see, no other country sails eggs. But maybe, McMary, some day it will catch on in other countries and islands and truly become the international sporting event it deserves to be.

"McMary, you've asked several times how I got my name, The Viscount. Now I shall tell you. It was after I had won the egg sailing competition in our Master's Roundabout, that is the journey between the Isle of

Goda down to Punta Arenas, Chile, by the Straights of Magellan, and back. Two hundred hyper class egg sailors went on that journey. Unfortunately, because of terrible weather at the bottom of the earth, we lost four egg sailors. The rest of us made it back and I was fortunate enough to come in first place in the greatest of all races at Goda. With that, I was conferred the title The Viscount, a title I shall carry for life.

"My real name is Derry Byrdseeder, taken from my father's partial Surinami last name, Borisfalter Byrdseederwaterfeeder. My first name is from my mother's partial last name Derrydingle-esche. She had some French Cajun blood in her. But back to the meaning of the egg...

"To our people, the egg is the greatest figment of nature. It is where all people come from you know, all animals as well, even the amphibians. Think about it, my love, all but plants come from eggs. This is God's way of saying what is important in life. When I was a little boy, I had read about Key West. I knew it was a sacred place because, as with beds and breakfasts, Key West has more chickens per capita than any place on earth. Think of it, McMary, my love, chickens are the greatest resplendent examples of the wonderment of eggs."

"Why, sir The Viscount, could it be that eggs are so important beyond anything else?"

"Because, my love, they are shaped so well, so strong, look so good, are a package unto themselves and, also, and this is God's doing, they do not hurt the chicken when they come out."

"You are so brilliant and so succinct at the same time," said McMary, who was now wishing The Viscount would take off his Brazilian admiral's jacket with the epaulets, his gray flannel shorts and cowboy boots, his matador's hat, too, and get randy with her. She was ready. He was not. This was a time to be voluble.

"I am so intrigued by this story, and I want to know where the Isle of Goda is; it sounds so far away. I hope you will tell, but first let's do more than just kiss; let's do the deed!" said McMary with an air of some frustration in her voice.

"My love, we have known each other with great passion for the last two weeks, as you say a long time in Key West. I shall tell you now from whence I came," The Viscount asserted.

"I wish to hear this so very much," said McMary, "but, but, but can't we make love now? We've waited so long."

"My beautiful flower, my garden of love, please, please, let us wait until I can provide, once again, better accommodations."

"Sir, The Viscount, I understand. I know what you wish to do at this time and it is more important than making love. It is telling me more about where you're from."

"It is time that you should know more details. I tell very few people, only those I am especially close to. For fear of ridicule and jest I suppose but my story is a true one and I believe it breeds inspiration and purpose especially in Key West, the Conch Republic, whose slogan, and properly so, is 'We Are One Human Family.'"

"You are so sensitive for a man, what a man, what a love," said McMary.

"Well, then, here is my story. I know you, McMary, will appreciate it more than most. It is my story and my journey.

"My father is of Surinami descent, but he grew up in Parma Heights, in Ohio. My mother is from Daphney, Alabama, a small town near Mobile. They met at a religious festival in Pumphrey, Alabama.

"Both my parents are entrepreneurs at heart, but first my father, and my mother agreed because she loved him so, that he should follow his dream."

McMary intoned, "What, The Viscount, my love was that dream?"

"His dream, and this actually happened, was to be the best stand-up comic in the Borscht Belt in the 1930s. He accomplished that, my good old dad, Zion. But first he had to earn his spurs in Missouri and my mother and he had a little deli in Cape Girardeau to make ends meet. Hannah and Zion worked hard together so that he could fulfill his dream, and like Count Basie, they had to spend their time in Missouri before they could cut the mustard in New York.

"You'd like my mother and my father, who by the way is a distant cousin to Elie Wiesel of Romania, who won a Pulitzer Prize for writing."

"What an amazing family," said McMary. "Please tell me more. Please."

"Well, after my father made it big in show business in the Poconos and later at Grossinger's at the epicenter of the Borscht Belt, the place where all the great comedians had come from – I'm talking Georgie Jessel, George Burns, Jerry Lewis, Myron Cohen, I'm talking the best – he chucked it all and went south. He had been offered a job on network TV but a guy named Jack Carter took it instead. It was one of the first comedy shows on television."

"Honey, why did your father do that, what with so much talent?" asked McMary.

"Because some guy at Grossinger's – I believe it was Morrie the maitre de – tipped him off to an opportunity.

"So my dad and mom went down to Suriname in South America and started a rice farm. And that's why I've been able to live with such abundance. They export to all over the world.

"When things really started happening for my family, we moved to the Isle of Goda, just off the coast of Suriname. What a place. The place looks like Pound Ridge, New York. Big homes. Big lawns. Long white fences. Ostriches."

"Ostriches? Why ostriches?" asked McMary.

"Well, they aren't the big ostriches, they are pygmies, about four feet high."

"And they produced eggs," said McMary.

"Oh, yes," said The Viscount.

"It turns out that Goda is the best place in the world for raising pygmy ostriches. Their eggs have eggs within them, kind of like a caviar. A real delicacy. On Goda these birds last a good 100 years and they are revered," The Viscount continued.

"The Isle of Goda is a special place; it is a Camelot. We have no crime, no lawyers, no laws, no courts, no police, no trouble."

"So why would you want to leave?" asked McMary.

"Well, the Isle of Goda has less than 10,000 inhabitants, although there could be as many as 100,000 pygmy ostriches there and an assortment of osprey and wildebeests and a variety of parakeets. It is a small island of small things, except the houses.

"And, I should add, my parents wanted me to see many of the other variances in life. As a child and an adult I have read extensively of Key West. I especially wanted to see Casa Antigua at 314 Simonton, where the Great Hemingway wrote A Farewell To Arms while he was nestled in the beautiful arms of Pauline Pieffer, who was soon to become his second wife. When we rode by the beautiful cream stucco and brown-trimmed building the other day, I felt myself falling back into history, a history so romantic. When we looked up at Hemingway's apartment, the first place he lived in Key West, Key West resolved itself into everything I had ever envisioned."

"The Viscount, you have never told me why you use a tall unicycle as your means of street travel," said McMary.

"My father got the idea when he was a comedian in the Borscht Belt. Guys would ride unicycles as part of the vaudevillian acts that would accompany him on stage. He especially liked the high ones, though they were difficult to maneuver until you had acquired a certain skill set.

"My father took to riding the nine-footer in Suriname to survey his abundant rice crops. He would say 'you can see anything from on high.' And this is true. I've been able to see a Key West from a special perspective.

"My father taught me how to ride and for this I shall ever be thankful. On the Isle of Goda we have no wires. In Key West I have to be more delicate, for I could fall on my arse if I don't watch out."

McMary replied, "You are a delicate man in every way, now can we… ?"

"In due course, my love. In due course."

And with that The Viscount fell back to sleep on the skanky mattress on the floor of the ramshackle house. But better things were to come.

❀

CHAPTER FIFTEEN

A Smoking Cigar

Morky Golub and Seamus Fine were having lunch at B.O.'s Fish Wagon with Rabbi Otto Blintz, their spiritual leader and a sage old man if there ever was one.

Their were talking about – what else – the ongoing but failing efforts by the authorities to piece together who killed Costas Delupas and what had happened to Heidi Hamm and Johnny Gordon. They didn't agree for one moment that the scoundrel was the midget plumber with one arm, Zero Belinsky.

As they each ate their grilled grouper sandwiches – maybe the best fish sandwiches in the world – and consumed a plate and a half of the freshly cut French fries, they offered their opinions. A few tables back from them, in the corner, was a young boy – maybe seven or eight – who was enjoying himself as well. The round-faced lad with the shock of black hair was sitting back in his chair in a most relaxed position, blowing smoke rings from a cigar. What? A cigar?? That's right a cigar!! And he knew how to hold it as well, not like some of the tourons who frequent K.W., walking down the streets with their cigars squarely in the center of their mouths, looking as if to impress passersby but instead just showing what idiots they are and how unsophisticated they are.

No, this young lad knew what he was doing and certainly enjoying it as well. The cigar looked to be expensive and large in size, maybe an El Presidente. The boy seemed to smirk at the customers who would look at him with chagrin. He didn't care and this was probably something he had been doing for quite some time, after lunching.

Rabbi Blintz noticed the boy first and then mentioned him to his luncheon partners. Nobody said anything about the boy; they just looked in awe, with their jaws dropped open, and then continued in their conversation. All three, having been in Key West for more than 20 years, just took it as just another form of the town's forever-quirky status.

"First of all, da moider and da meesing couple are kee-nected," retorted Rabbi Blintz.

"Morky and I agree with you there," responded Seamus Fine, not really having any reason or evidence to say that.

"It's somebody we know, all right," expressed Morky.

"Has to be for shoi," shot back the rabbi in his Hassidic dialect. He too had grown up in the Williamsburg section of Brooklyn, New York, but a generation before Morky Golub and Seamus Fine. Mostly these three men found common ground. Their families had pretty much all come from the hat making business for which the Williamsburg section is renowned. And the Key West heat didn't keep the rabbi from wearing his top hat and long beard. Morky and Seamus found comfort in this because it gave them a good link back to their rich ethnic past, though it looked strange in this Caribbean clime.

"Vat you tink, boys? Maybe we shoid pay Zero Belinsky a visit at the Monroe County Detention Center, and the Sheriff's headquarters. Vat are friends for?" asked the rabbi. "Vhen he was a boyee he alwavys vent to synagogue, and he listened too. Not like some of the people of today, you know. Zero eeeze a good boyee even today, vhat vith his double handicap. How many people could accompleesh so much vith having the distraction of beeeing a midget and having just vone arm? He does have two stomachs dough. Dat vas da one good ting dat happened from da Thalidamide.

"He eeze not only a plumber but a good plumber, handling some amazing jobs just any plumber could not do. He is a skeeled craftsman with vath he does. And just bee-cause he lookie likes Oy-nest Hemingvay, people, they take hee-em for granted. You know, these cops, they good cops, but they may try to railroading hee-em. Den, vat happ-eeens, our good friend go to jail for good. Ka-put. Spritch."

So the three made it their duty to visit Zero Belinsky.

❋

They were led into the visitors' room at the Monroe County Detention Center, up on Stock Island. As they entered, they could see Zero Belinsky sitting on the other side of the glass – on three or four Miami phone books.

Belinksy was weeping and drawing deep sobs.

"I didn't kill Costas. I don't know what happened to Johnny. Maybe Heidi wanted to elope with him. That's what I think, but now they have me charged with one crime and have me as the lead suspect in the disappearance. Rabbi Blintz, I was schtupping Heidi when Johnny came back to the boat that night. I couldn't have felt worse for Johnny. I shouldn't have done that but I was horny after a long and bad day at work.

"I know-wa, I know-wa," said the rabbi. "Vee vill try to hel-leep you. Vee vill, I am sure of dat. Von't vee, boys?"

Morky and Seamus nodded in agreement but had no idea of what they were going to do to save the midget.

"The best thing that can happen, Zero, is if the Sheriff's office comes up with another suspect or more," said Seamus.

"Yes, but (sobs), they may just be satisfied with me," said Zero. "Why (sobbing) are they going to try to find anyone else now, when they have me?" (farting out of nervousness)

Seamus said, "You can't put yourself in the position of feeling sorry for yourself. You have to be alert. We have to be alert, too. We're convinced that the killer is somebody on the island, probably somebody we know."

"But you do agree (sobbing) it isn't me?" (farting)

"Oh, sweet justice, vee do," said the rabbi. "Keep thinking of who else eeet it could have bee-en. Ple-eeze do that's for you-self. Ple-eeze. I can understand vhy they vould have you under soos-peecion for da disappearance of Johnny Gordon and his goilfriend but not fors DeLupas. No vay, Jose.

"Vee have hoid there is a dee-tective from Philly they call Obretta who has other people under suspicion on these cases but can't do nuttin because he's retired. He suspects everyone, according to an article in da *Citizen*. But he eeze usually vrong, like da *Citizen* eeze usually vrong and every other goddamn newspaper eeze usually wrong but may-beee he vill devote da time to help us."

So then the three decided to look up Obretta, who they heard was staying at the Truman Annex. They left little Zero on the other side of the plexiglas weeping, sobbing... and farting.

Ted and his friends were staying in a big house across the street from the Mill's Place section of the annex. They were lounging around the small pool in the backyard, after being thrown out of the much bigger pool at Mill's Place. It seems that the neo-Nazis who run the tenants' association at the annex have a rule that you must only use the pool assigned to the section in which you are staying. There was no one else at the Mill's Place pool at the time of their banishment, just the four friends, Whit Wyatt, Zemblon Yurcocitch, Charlie York and Ted Obretta.

Because of their unceremoniously obnoxious exit from the big pool and gardens at Mill's Place, the four came up with a new name for the beautiful but rigid area of Key West known as the Truman Annex, part of the old Naval yards during World War II and the Korean War. They started calling it the "Anal Annex." "So this is what we get for $5000 a week?" said Whitlow sarcastically.

One of the homeowners nearby told them that the place has gotten so rigid that you must obtain approval from the association to put up "just the right kind" of lights ornamenting your house or condo during the Christmas season.

His buddies were also kidding Ted unmercifully about his "gumshoes" propensity during their seven-day vacation. The last several days they had hardly seen him because he was spending so much time on the Delupas and Gordon cases.

"You go to Key West, America's Caribbean paradise, and you spend more than half your time tracking down leads that are going nowhere fast," said Whitlow Wyatt, who was spending enough of his own time away with his new girlfriend from Kato, Iowa: Pansy Riviera. Well, unfortunately a good deal of that time they spent together was with the investigators in the Delupas case, seeing as it was the lovers who discovered his body.

Whit needed a break, even from Pansy, and wanted to be with his friends and laugh it up a bit.

The other two guys, Yurcocitch and York pretty much continued to do what they do best, continue a week-long buzz, hitting all the local and touristo bars with relish.

Zemblon Yurcocitch, the podiatrist, and Charlie York, the PR man, were seriously considering becoming members of the Conch Republic, a country-state some 20 years old and dedicated to the good life. The Conch Republic has its generals and admirals and other officers and is infused with the credo that "we all are part of the same human family." The Conch Republic, for about fifty dollars, even issues passports that are notarized and recognized by a couple of dozen other countries around the world. If you want to spend some more money you can even get a diplomatic passport that will enable you to be whisked through airports without any of the folderol that the peons have to endure. You move right through security checkpoints without waiting in line and you are accorded the finest treatment that only the diplomatic corps and some certain celebrities receive. And it's all for a good cause: promoting world peace, happiness and understanding… and also having a good time.

So this afternoon, after some sun and suds Yurcocitch and York will head down to the Conch Republic headquarters at 611 Whitehead Street to be sworn in as Conch citizens. The last thing they want to do is get caught up with a murder case, in Ted's case, or a girl in Whitlow Wyatt's. No, they are here to have a good time, the good time General Jeff of the Conch Republic Army talked about at the Pier House's Chart Room Bar, a very small, dark bar with peanut shells on the floor. A bar that used to be a hotel room, a small hotel room, at one time.

Just as he was about to have some R & R for the first time in three days, Ted Obretta was alerted to the doorbell in their sumptuous rented home in the annex.

Ted had a hunch it was one of the Sheriff's deputies maybe telling him to bug off the Delupas and Gordon cases. Maybe, maybe not. After all he was a big city detective accustomed to solving many homicides. But that wasn't the way it works in Key West or Monroe County. Those departments didn't need or want the help. They already were dealing with the FBI, the state investigators, the Federal Bureau of Alcohol, Tobacco and Firearms, the Coast Guard and the Naval police.

To Ted's dismay it was a rabbi and two younger

men on the threshold of his rented house.

'What is going on here?' Ted wondered as he said hello.

"Are you Ted Obretta from Pheely-delphia? Vee have seen you photo in the newspapers. Vee read about you in da *Citizen* and *Key West,* da *Newspaper*," said the rabbi. "Vee sorely need your help."

❋

CHAPTER SIXTEEN

Finally, They Get It Down

IT WAS PAST 3 A.M. in the morning. Most of the habitues of Duval Street were long in their beds, but some rowdies persisted. There is a little bar between Greene and Front streets, on the south side of Duval. A very little bar. You see, it only has two seats.

Appropriately, it is called "The Smallest Bar In The World." There may be only two seats but sometimes, though, there are a lot more people in that bar than you would think. The bartender says that he has had as many as 70 partiers in the joint at one time, which would be quite a feat, since there is not much frontage from the bar and the street. The only way this could be done is to have the revelers stack up down the lane behind the bar. The lane is attached to a quaint little inn, above and around the bar.

So on this day, past 3 a.m., there are only four people having their good time. Most incredibly, two of them are having some masterful sex right on one of the two stools. The bartender watches and kibitzes with them and the one other patron, a bearded gent of middle age, with a long-beaked fisherman's cap on, a Green Parrot shirt and some long green bathing shorts as the rest of his ensemble. This group, of course, was well into their oats at this time of the early morning.

An occasional passerby, in a similar condition, would cross the opening to the bar and sometimes look in. It must have been a sight, but, then, the bar is so small that it could go largely unnoticed. It's the type of bar that you'd have to be looking for to find.

Strange thing that not only the couple and the bartender but also the fiftyish man were engaged in frequent and boisterous conversation, all the while the hetero couple were doing it with half their clothes on. They were getting to know each other in a Key West kind of way.

At one point, the bartender chided the guy doing it. The bartender said he could do it better, with a better technique, at which point the bartender bolted around the little bar and started amorously kissing the girl about the face and neck and grabbed some feels as well.

Her partner then returned to action and now she seemed to be enjoying an even more feverish pleasure.

The older guy just looked on in meditation and, of course, at the sight of the fervor, occasionally commenting.

As they went about their amour, the couple conversed with the bartender and the bearded gent.

It was all very strange.

The sounds, especially.

"Anybody know if the Twins won last night."

"Squish, squash, squish, eww, eee, ahhh, ohhhh, yeah."

"Way to go, baby!" (in the Mike Myers manner)

"The Twins did not win last night; they were beaten by the Indians."

"Too bad."

"Scree, squish, squash, urgh, urgh, urgh, cachoo, eee, yoy, cachoo, cachoo, squish, squish, hubba, hubba, ohmygod, yeah, yeah, oh yeah."

Ah, the sounds of love. The sounds of conversation.

"Ya, think it'll rain tomorrow?"

"Da-know?"

"What's the best place to get some around here?"

"Right here, right here. The girl's in heat!"

"Squash, squash, squeezze, urgh, eee, cachoo, cachoo, bubba, bubba, bubba, goyyyyyy, squish, squish, squish, oh no, no, no, yes, yes, yes, ohhhhhhh yeahhhhhh, squish, squeezeee, spunka, spunka, cachoo, ha, ha, ha, wooza, wooza, cachoo, yeahhhh, yeahhhhhh, yeahhhhhh, oh, oh, oh magod, oh, more, more, squissssssssh, squisssssssh, plot, wooza, yeah, yeah, hubba, emmmh, emmmh, yezzzzzz, whoooopa, whoooopa, squisssssssshs, oooooooohhhhhh,
that's it, that's it, that's it oooohhhhhhhhh, yessssss, yessss, ohhhohhoohohhhoohooooho. That was good."

"You could have done better," chided the bartender to the male partner. "You need to take lessons from me, or, better, just watch me some time. How 'bout right now when she is hot and heavy?"

Meanwhile, the other customer asked if he should turn left or right to get to the Schooner Wharf.

The couple was Whit Wyatt and his new girlfriend, Pansy Riviera, from Kato, Iowa.

"God, you girls from Iowa really know how to do it," Whitlow said to Pansy.

"Thank you, but you know I'm really from California, and, by the way, you guys from Buffalo know how to do it too.

They held arms around each other as they coursed

down Duval back to the Wicker Inn where she was staying. There would be more tonight.

They deserved it, for they had spent a good 14 hours at the Monroe County Sheriff's Department that day and the day and early evening before. They had finally consummated their friendship on a stool in "The World's Smallest Bar," a consummation that had started with some idle kissing that erupted into pawing and mashing, more drinks, and the deed itself. Ahhhhh, life is good – eventually.

Meanwhile, the other patron from the Smallest Bar ambled his way down Greene Street across the harbor deck and into the Schooner Wharf, a favorite place for the late, late night crowd. Well, the early crowd and the midday and evening crowd as well.

He sat down on a chair next to a distinguished man with a macaw on his shoulder.

The gentleman with the bird introduced himself and his bird, which was talking louder than he was. "My name is Ubi Ubi, from the country of Ubi and this is my macaw, Filigree. Excuse me if he talks too much. He does that when he is tired or mad about something. He swears a bit too. I just wanted to warn you."

A couple chairs down on the other side of Ubi, Ubi, the premier of his country, sat two men who looked rough and tumble. Real bad asses.

They were staring daggers at the bird, which had a helmet of black and gold feathers on its head but neck down it was denuded. Quite a sight. But the bikers on the left were pissed off at the bird's incessant jabbering and screaming. They certainly didn't understand that Ubi Ubi and Filigree had just arrived in Key West from a trip around the world, from their home country of Ubi.

The bearded man on the right immediately recognized Ubi Ubi from all the press he had received last year. The man remembered when the United Nations honored Ubi Ubi for his unstinting leadership against predators who were trying to gain control of his country. Premier Ubi had been on TV and in the papers for weeks as coverage of the revolt by his people against the intruders intensified. He knew Ubi Ubi to be a man of peace and honor and he wanted to shake the hand of the man who saved his country, located just below China on the Yellow Sea and just west of Dalian.

The bearded gent leaned over to shake Ubi Ubi's hand to congratulate him on his successful efforts at fending off the predators – the Holy See, the E. H. Meris pharmaceutical company and a band of Texas real estate developers, the story of which is chronicled in another journal.

But Premier Ubi Ubi did not shake hands. Rather, he crossed his arms in the Ubian manner, and the man with the beard folded his own arms across to return the gesture. In Ubi it is thought the shaking of hands is unhealthy and so the crossing of arms is the manner in which Ubians greet each other and those from other coutries.

"Thank you. I always feel at home here in Key West. The officials of our government and I often like to vacation here," said Premier Ubi. "But it is a long journey from our country to the keys. Takes a day of travel, yet I always find it worth it. And one of my favorite places is the Schooner Wharf, which is always open late and we can unwind after our trip."

While Premier Ubi and the bearded man were exchanging pleasantries, one of the bikers on the left turned again and scowled at the bird.

"Fuck you, fat boy!" ripped the macaw.

"Look, buddy, tell that little sonbitch to shut up, or I'm going to snap his neck in two and cook him for lunch tomorrow," yelled the biker at Ubi Ubi.

The older man with the salt and pepper beard and stocky 5-10 build walked past Premier Ubi and over to the biker and tried to calm him down. The well-built blond Adonis of a bartender stepped in as well.

"He means no harm," said Ubi of the bird. "We will just leave if he is bothering you. He's just tired and touchy. I'll take him back to the Pier House.

"Fuck you, fat boy!" screeched Filigree as Ubi Ubi got up to leave the bar.

The biker appeared to have been lurching for the bird, when a strong arm grabbed him around the neck and threw him to the dirt floor. It was the left arm of Ted Obretta. The burly ex-Philly detective had been sitting at the other side of the bar observing the goings on at the Schooner, but especially he was casing the two bikers, in his voluntary quest to solve the Delupas murder case. Ted recognized Premier Ubi as well and wanted to make sure he and the bird weren't hurt.

A statesman, two bikers, a bearded gentleman who had just watched two people copulating at another bar, a denuded loud-mouth bird, and an ex-detective on a mission. Late night. Trouble in the air. Police sirens. Just another night in the Conch Republic.

❇

CHAPTER SEVENTEEN

Balloons Bursting All Over

Key West likes to take pride in taking pride. A good example is PrideFest, which takes place each year in early June. It is an assemblage of the K.W. culture, including art and crafts showcases, lots of music and performance, food and drink. Largely founded and carried forward by the gay community, starting originally on a small lane and now in all its glory at the center of Duval Street, it is open to all souls who wish to have a good time. It has actually turned into a family affair, drawing a few thousand people – locals and visitors alike – to what Key Westers share warmly under their motto of "One Human Family." They like to show the world the liberation of living in an open and tolerant community. And that is cool.

One of the signatures of PrideFest is its multi-colored balloon arbors arching from one curb to the other high over Duval and repeating several times over the multi-block gala.

So it was with great gusto that The Viscount rode down Duval toward the festival, with the lovely raven-haired McMary Marimba trailing behind him on a normal bicycle. The Viscount rode proudly toward PrideFest, smoking a fine El Presidente cigar, wearing his ever-on double-breasted blue blazer with the epaulets, his gray-flannel shorts and yellow cowboy boots. He was also sporting his red poppy, his pencil thin mustachio and a floppy Panama hat with a carmine band around it. He was ever so careful to take white poppies – though poppies do come in red hues – and soak them in maraschino juices until they became a combination of red with white edges of the petals. The Viscount was in joy this beautiful Saturday afternoon.

As he pedaled on his nine-foot-high unicycle so assuredly and happily something unfortunate happened. He was beginning to look back for his girlfriend and as he turned his head (which is not recommended while riding a unicycle) at Olivia and Duval, his well-lit cigar brushed up against one of the balloons on the first arbor, and popped the balloon. Then, while he fell down sideways, several others exploded causing a machine gun effect that startled the crowd. On top of that one of the balloons caught fire and not but seconds later the entire arbor was ablaze. Not a true problem, but causing much alarm to the guests and especially the PrideFest organizers and some of their exhibitors nearby.

By now, all of the balloons were popping or had popped, an unwanted cacophony at this festive occasion. Not to say the least of which was the destruction of the first arbor where guests entered. That end of the multi-block festival was shortly into chaos. And now The Viscount was getting up from the street and apologizing profusely as McMary brushed him off.

"It certainly was not my intention to harm this party," The Viscount explained to the organizers. "I was just trying to see where McMary was behind me and when I looked back, I suddenly realized that I had gone on too far forward and had stricken the arch. I am so sorry."

He was explaining himself to Key West police officers who were standing nearby. They were further annoyed because he had ridden between two barricades that were set up to prevent vehicular traffic from coming down Duval. And by now, several squad cars had arrived.

McMary, wearing a white-trimmed red halter-top and white shorts, tried in vain to explain to the officers that it was an accident. But they weren't buying anything. They had been watching this strange bird, who called himself The Viscount, for days. They were suspicious of this newcomer to K.W. and they were waiting for him to make a mistake. Now he had. And they hauled him into the jail at police headquarters on Angela Street. They were determined to know more about him, and they would be charging him with vehicular recklessness and arson. Woe is The Viscount.

In the next holding cell were Gary Bluett and Artie Pepico. They were not happy. They had been apprehended at PrideFest as suspects in the Delupas murder because rat poison had been found in their garage alongside their little conch bungalow on Shavers Lane. Someone had tipped the police off, and while the Monroe County Sheriff's Department was investigating the case because it had implications beyond the city limits, the K.W. police had stepped in because Bluett and Pepico lived in Key West proper.

And now it had become known from the coroner that Delupas had succumbed to a poisonous substance and that substance was rat poison. How his body got up to the submarine slips in the mangroves was a question that hadn't been answered. Lovie Jones, the Sheriff's deputy on the case for the county, had stopped by to chat with the Key West police on this afternoon. Jones was a thick-armed, bull-necked black man who wanted to solve this case on his own. He was not about to give way to the police unless he absolutely had to. He was thinking that there could be plenty of other suspects out there, "besides these two twinkies," as he referred to them in a later phone conversation he had with Ted Obretta, who originally thought they were suspects but now had changed his mind. This case was getting confusing, Ted had helped confuse it, and now all Lovie was trying to do was keep it all within his control.

Gary Bluett, a slight blond, had been in Key West for about eight years now. He hailed from Huddleton, Indiana, a town that had no toleration for his kind. His partner, Artie Pepico, had been here about a year. He's from Rye, New York. Artie's part Puerto Rican and part

Italian, and also slender and short but with jet black hair.

Sergeant Farley Cosmass had been interviewing these guys for the last couple of hours and remained fairly convinced that they were implicated in the death of Costas Delupas, but, unfortunately just finding rat poison in someone's garage doesn't necessarily implicate the suspect in a crime. Afterall, the rat poison could have been planted by someone else, perhaps the killer, who liked neither Delupas nor Bluett/Pepico. Or, and was this the bigger question, was the poison simply there for the killing of rats? Mind boggling.

"We hardly know Costas Delupas," said Bluett to Cosmass. "We used to go in his store once every couple of months. He had good stuff but we weren't too sure he liked us. He was kind of a prejudiced guy. Don't think he liked gays very much. We preferred to stay away from him. Why would we have killed him? Nothing to gain."

"Well and good, but just what did you go in there to buy? You must have known he was a light dealer of drugs – all the crap. Nobody could ever catch him. We think he was done in by one or more of his customers or by the drug people he dealt with," Sergeant Cosmass had told the two.

Angrily, Artie Pepico, lashed back and said, "Listen, asshole, we are not guilty as sin. We are just two gay guys who would prefer to mind our own business. You guys pick us right off the street in the middle of PrideFest, for which we devoted hours of our time, and we now spend the whole Fest in jail. We're probably going to miss the parade, too, which is stepping off at 7 p.m.

sharp. We're pissed and you better know it buster."

"Look you little bastard spic fruit, you and your buddy aren't going anywhere any time soon," shrieked Sergeant Farley Cosmass, a big fat guy who had been on the force for more than 20 years.

"You look, fat ass, I grew up in Rye, New York. I'm sure I know a lot more than a moron like you. You can't catch the real killers so you pick on us," Artie yelled, as his friend Gary Bluett hung his head. Bluett was usually the one doing the talking for the two.

❈

The Viscount gasped at what he was hearing. He could only assume what would be in store for him. But an hour later, the police let him go, not even spending any time to interrogate him. Someone had sprung him. He thought it must have been McMary, but he was wrong. She had gone for help but had not yet found it. No, this was someone else who had an interest in The Viscount, someone else who persuaded them that his setting fire to the big balloon arbor at PrideFest was an accident. That someone had a good reason for springing The Viscount.

As he hopped back on his nine-foot high unicycle he just assumed it was McMary and he raced up to their shambles of a manse on Duval, at the corner of United, to thank her.

❈

CHAPTER EIGHTEEN

Who Got The Viscount Out Of Jail?

McMary, in a panic, had raced over to Pearl's Patio, a handsome little pool bar, behind Pearl's Rainbow Inn on United. She knew that organizers of PrideFest might be there and she wanted to see if she could plead with them to drop any charges against The Viscount.

Shallaha Oobst and Charla Severan were at their usual perches at the bar. In the pool nearby another lesbian couple were getting exceedingly romantic. But they did not draw Shallaha's or Charla's notice, for they were busy paying attention to each other and to their mojitoes, those great Cuban drinks favored by Hemingway.

McMary ran up to them from the Inn's center hall in a panic.

"Please, please, I need your help with The Viscount.

He's in jail and the police are not in a good mood about his crashing into the arbor at PrideFest. He is a good man and would never damage a thing on purpose. He was just looking out for me, making sure I was riding behind him. You know he's a gentle soul. I'm just afraid they're going to throw him off the island and send him back home."

"Look, girl, we saw what happened. We believe you, McMary. I think the police have just been tense because this is the first time PrideFest was this big, and on Duval St. for the first time. We'll go down to the police station with you and help you get him out of there. There are plenty of our friends who will do the same," said Charla.

"No one is going to press charges," chimed in Shallaha. Why don't you have a mojito with us and calm yourself down? Why don't you have a few before we go over to the police station?"

"O.K.," said McMary. "But I can't let that beautiful gentleman stay in jail too long. Where he is from they don't have jails and they don't have crime. He doesn't understand all this. He's very sensitive, wouldn't hurt a gnat. He's the kind of person we need more of in Key West. The Viscount stands for all that the Conch Republic stands for. He believes in one human family. He fully subscribes to the Conch Republic's ethos as the world's first fifth world nation existing as a sovereign state of mind. That's the Key West he has come to know and love. Like Key West, known to us as the Conch Republic, he seeks only to bring more humor, warmth and respect to a planet that needs all three.

"He even just obtained his Conch Republic passport, which is recognized by more than 30 countries, including the U.S., Ireland, Mexico, Sweden, Cuba, Ecuador, Germany, Spain, and I think Estonia and Suriname," McMary breathlessly continued. "He's a Conch in spirit, mind and body. He could be the president of the Conch Republic for all which it stands."

"Hold down, girl, hold down," said Charla. "We're with you and The Viscount. We'll get him out of jail."

"See, here's his Conch passport," said McMary. "He asks me to carry it and his money for him because his grey flannel shorts are too tight and they encumber him when he rides high on his unicycle."

"Not a nobler man there is," said Shallaha. "Let's get some of the organizers of the PrideFest and go over to Angela St. and get him out of the hoosgow."

To their surprise there was no The Viscount to be had at the city jail. Sergeant Cosmass told them he had been released and the charges had been dropped.

"Who got him out?" questioned McMary, concerned for his welfare.

"I can't tell you that, lady. That's official and confidential information."

"Where did he go? Where did he go?"

"I hope he went back to Pluto, lady. He's one weird dude. Believe me, we'll get him out of here one way or another. He'll make another mistake, and we're just watching for it," chortled Sergeant Cosmass. We've got enough weird asses here already. He makes Fantasy Fest at Halloween look normal by comparison. Maybe the cops will accept him at Provincetown, but not here."

Shallaha, Charla and McMary left the police station and headed up to the dilapidated house on Duval and United looking for him.

※

They found The Viscount sitting on a rickety chair on the front porch. He was sitting there still with his Brazilian admiral's jacket on and now his felt musketeer's hat atop his head. His red poppy in the lapel was going limp in the 92-degree heat. Thank God he wasn't wearing a shirt beneath the jacket. Even though The Viscount was through and through a man of Key West, he still had an air of formality about him, the only concession being his gray flannel cuffed shorts. And he still had on his heavy riding boots.

"Who, my dear, came to get you out of jail?" asked McMary.

"I don't know, sweet. One officer indicated it was a tall, slender man who was quite bandaged up. He wouldn't give me the man's name or any other details," said The Viscount.

With that, The Viscount grabbed McMary and pulled her to him lustily. He squeezed her hard about the waist and noshed her ruby red lips with drippy passion. All this on the broken down wicker chair on their front porch. Shallaha and Charla took the hint and slipped down the stairs back to Pearl's Patio where they would be more comfortable with their Lesbian friends.

Oh, yessiree, The Viscount had chosen this time to take McMary Marimba and as he proceeded to the next steps on in the carnal journey, he began an endless string of major league farts, sounding much like a fireworks display.

"It's the Cuban beans from last night at Jose's Cantina. I'm awfully sorry," said The Viscount, somewhat hiding his head under his armpit.

"Don't worry, my love, this is our moment," said McMary.

❇

CHAPTER NINETEEN

Romance Into The Night

THAT AFTERNOON OVER AT the broken down house on Duval and United, The Viscount and the scrumptious McMary Marimba continued their release of tension from his brief jailing by banging, banging and banging, until the wicker chair broke in half.

That night after a couple of drinks at Donnie's on Simonton, predominantly a gay bar populated by men of all ages but also some heteros and gay ladies, the two went to the San Carlos Institute. There they saw William Shatner do his schtick along with big time singer wannabe Brian Evans. Evans, who is a good singer in his own rank, having come from Las Vegas and Hollywood not so long ago, is now putting on shows at the San Carlos featuring stars such as Wayne Newton, Joan Rivers and Shatner wherein they just perform the best of their acts. In other words, Newton would sing stuff like Danke Schoen and other hits and that's about it.

Shatner told some odd stories about Star Trek, sang a bit and did some hoofing. An actor and a TV pitchman for various products, he was easily outdone by Evans, who thinks he might be a crooner of proportions that could make him the next Sinatra.

While all this was going on, McMary and The Viscount cuddled in the beautiful and capacious theater where every seat is a good one. The Spanish stucco theatrical house has plenty of character and is another good example of the many cultural amenties in the Conch Republic.

Afterwards, the couple gravitated over to a place called Hula's. It's on Petronia, south of Duval Street. Things get under way there later in the evening. It's a place where, shall we say, you can really get it on. That is, couples in various curtained alcoves have some fun getting to know each other or getting to know each other better. The Viscount and McMary found their own little nook and continued their romantic cavalcade in hot and heavy form.

If that were not enough, they later decided to look at the fulsome moon that night and went over to the Key West cemetary off of Olivia Street to do so. Oh, sure, it was a romantic night, especially now that it had started to rain, a fine kind of misty rain, as grayish moonlit clouds moved in from the Gulf. It was beginning to cool down the hot air, but not much, and certainly not for McMary and The Viscount.

"It is so white, so big," said McMary as they

looked up to the sky and as the moon made errie shadows on the graves, most of which were above ground, some stacked.

Many of the famed characters and personages of Key West lore, going back a couple hundred years were buried there. The Porters, the Currys, the Mallorys, the Greenes, "Sloppy Joe" Russell, Senator John Spottswood, Elfina (the key deer who was the family pet of the Ottos from 1941 to 1956), Bolo Godinet (who delivered newspapers in Key West for 64 years) and Edwina Lariz ("Devoted fan of Julio Iglesias") are among the hundreds resting comfortably in these quaint confines.

It wasn't long before The Viscount got another glint in his eye on this increasingly drizzly night. He pulled McMary atop a three-stacked coffin condo and the day and evening of wacky whacking continued into the sleepy hours of the night.

"This cemetery is so romantic, my dear," gurgled The Viscount, as the rain began coming down more heavily.

While all this lovemaking was going on, the relentless Ted Obretta was hiding himself behind the grave of B. P. Roberts, 1929-1979, whose inscription simply states "I Told You I Was Sick." Ted was crouched down real low so the revelers could not possibly see him, though he could see them quite well.

He had heard about the jailing of The Viscount earlier in the day and he wondered why The Viscount was released and by whom. Perhaps both of these people – The Viscount and the man who got him released – could be connected to the Delupas murder and the missing Johnny Gordon and Heidi Hamm.

By now it was 2 a.m. and Ted only had two nights more to go on his vacation. He figured he might stay on a few days more to help settle the case. He called Lovie Jones, the Sheriff's deputy at home, to tell him about his latest observations. Jones was not too happy about being awakened in the hot night with the phone call, but then, realistically, he should have known better than to list himself in the Key West phone directory. Obretta had looked up Jones's number just before Obretta left his place in the Truman Annex. He figured it might be handy to have the phone number handy on this detail, and he wanted to help Lovie Jones as best he could so that Jones was clearly in control of the investigation and not the Key West police. Unfortunately, Jones just wished Ted Obretta would go away – go back to Philadelphia.

As Ted called in a whispered voice from his cell phone, Lovie Jones scowled, "Whatch you want now? Don't you know what time it is? I need some rest... these cases are driving me crazy and so are you."

"Just trying to help out, Lovie," said Obretta. Some interesting developments and I just want to pass on what I see."

"Whatch you see now, brother?"

"I see that McMary Marimba gal and that idiot, The Viscount, making out."

"Where you at, bro?" asked Deputy Sheriff Jones, sleepily.

"Whatch you watching them making out, bro? That's an invasion of privacy, bro. Whatch you some kind of voyeur or something? Next thing you're going to know is the po-leese are going to pick you up for being a peeping Tom. You gotta know better than that. You was one of the po-leese yourself. You are one crazy cat, brother."

"Hey, I'm just running a detail here at the cemetery," said Ted Obretta, the former Philly detective.

"What the hell you doin' at the cemetery? That place is closed up at dusk. You are violatin' the place. This time of night you should leave the dead be," yelled Lovie Jones into Ted's cell phone. "Don't you have any sense of shame?"

"No, no, you don't get it, you don't get it," whispered back Ted, afraid that his prey would find him out.

It was starting to rain quite heavily now and little rivulets of muddy water were flowing his way as Ted lay on the ground in his Tommy Bahama outfit, the shirt of which was so flowery that if he moved slightly he would be found out.

"Look, Lovie, they're up there screwing on top of three cemetery vaults, they're stacked three up and the suspects are on top. They're violating something here, too, buddy. Maybe I ought to call the police and have them arrested. Whadaya think?"

"First off, you are not a cop any more. You are flirtin' with trouble, bro. People make out in the cemetery all the time. We leave them alone, as long as they're not making a lot of noise or drinking. This is part of the Key West spirit, don't you know anything, brother?" screamed Deputy Sheriff Jones into the phone.

"I'm going to pretend I never got this call," he continued.

"No, wait," Ted whispered. "I was trying to overhear what they are saying. This could give us some leads. I'm not going to bother them, just try to get some information that 'ill help the case."

"Get out of there now, bro, or you going to get caught for being a pree-vert. The Key West cops patrol around the cemetery all night looking for people like you."

Seconds later a squad car came rumbling along Olivia Street, just to the east of the cemetery. This was its first pass around the burial grounds.

The Viscount and McMary didn't notice, and the cops in the car got a chuckle watching the two go at it.

Ted was flat on the ground behind the low slung grave top, now trying not to be seen by the couple and certainly not by the police. He crawled a few hundred feet over to a taller grave. It was in the Arnold family plot, next to the Taylor Tomb, where he was afforded more cover. By now, Ted's thick black-gray hair was matted with mud and his Tommy Bahama shirt and shorts looked like he had been playing in one of those muddy pickup rugby games of yore. At least he had good camouflage, he thought.

He could see that the cop car was moving around the corner from Olivia and then westward along Windsor Lane.

What Ted didn't see was there was now only one cop in the car.

The other one was approaching from behind, off Angela Street, with two other officers who had arrived in another cop car that had been parked under a tree on Grinnell, near Angela.

The first officer yelled to Ted Obretta to raise his hands above his head. All three officers had their pistols drawn, as the cop in the first police car, coming from the south side of the cemetery, put on his siren, called for more reinforcements, and screeched around the corner to assist with the arrest. Soon, there were five squad cars there.

The assumption was the suspect, former detective

Ted Obretta, was just one of several people, perhaps doing or selling drugs in the cemetery, or perhaps only a lone man who was a peeping Tom. They closed in.

Meanwhile, McMary and The Viscount scampered out of the cemetery down Packer Street and back to their home, where they made love one more time on the front porch, not even making it into the house.

❃

CHAPTER TWENTY

"Former Cop Arrested As Voyeur"

Ted Obretta had some explaining to do. Now the man who suspected everyone was, indeed, a suspect himself.

The next edition of *The Key West Citizen* had a front-page story about Ted's arrest. People around town got quite a chuckle out of the story. By the time the story appeared, Ted was out of jail, but still quite embarrassed by the incident at the cemetery.

Finally, upon reading the story and noting the time of the incident, McMary and The Viscount got the idea that someone had been watching them.

"We should be more careful, love," said McMary over coffee and blueberry waffles at Les Croissants des France. Many of the other patrons were reading the newspaper and laughing out loud and pointing it out to people at the other tables.

One guest, a white-bearded guy with short dark brown and grayish hair, asked his bespeckled friend who was dozing off and appeared to be a body builder or at least a former one, "I wonder who he was watching?"

These two guys were sitting right next to McMary and The Viscount. McMary turned crimson at the comment.

"Someone must have been putting on quite a show," the bearded guy said to his friend who had woken up, though briefly.

The Viscount was oblivious to these comments, as McMary grew redder.

After Ted had been hauled over to the police station in the middle of the night handcuffed, he explained who he was and what he was doing and the Key West officers were sympathetic. After all, he was of them or at least used to be.

He didn't have to do much explaining for them to believe him. And, of course, they were suspicious of the couple, after he described "this guy in a blue jacket with epaulets with his gray-flannel shorts down and wearing what appeared to be a musketeer's hat doing this girl with long black curly hair." They just knew it was the guy who called himself The Viscount, and they were growing ever more suspicious of this guy who had himself been in jail the previous day.

The police decided they would pay him a visit at his house on Duval at United. They wanted to further question The Viscount and also track down the slender tallish man in bandages who had come down to the jail to get The Viscount's release. Somehow, they thought, these two had something in common and they wanted to compare notes, thinking that the murder of Costas Delupas and the mysterious disappearance of Johnny Gordon and Heidi Hamm had occurred shortly after The Viscount's arrival in Key West. They were disturbed that the prime suspect had been arrested and incarcerated at the Monroe County Sheriff's detention center on Stock Island. The prime suspect being the one-armed midget plumber Zero Belinsky. They would like to settle this case on their terms, eradicating the Sheriff's own investigation.

The competition between these two law enforcement organizations had always been a stiff one.

By the time The Viscount and McMary had returned to their house, two squad cars were already waiting for them.

❊

Led by Sergeant Farley Cosmass, a half dozen Key West police officers descended upon the derelict little mansion on Duval at United. When they arrived, McMary and The Viscount were arm-in-arm, sitting akimbo on the rusted glider swing on the front porch. At first they hardly heard the herd of policemen storming toward their house.

"Excuse me, lady and gentleman, if I could have your attention for a moment, we have some questions for you. I hate to interrupt your caucus but this appears to be as good a time as any," Sergeant Cosmass said with his usual sarcasm.

"First of all, how well did you know Costas Delupas, the guy who was murdered, poisoned and thrown in the mangroves?"

As McMary and The Viscount uncoupled, McMary said, "I'm the one who knew him. I used to go to 'Taste of Bulgaria' at least a couple of times a week. My boyfriend here had only been there once, I think a day or two before Costas died."

McMary was wearing a deeply plunging purple haltertop with green short shorts. Sergeant Cosmass and his associates were salivating more than just from the 93-degree sun, Cosmass thinking 'where does this asshole weirdo get a broad like McMary?'

"Sir, tell me, what kind of drugs do you do?" asked Cosmass. You obviously are on something, maybe that's why you paid Delupas a visit."

"Sergeant Cosmass, I don't do drugs. I've never taken drugs, although I do like a stiff cocktail," responded The Viscount.

"Did you know that Costas Delupas was a small-time drug dealer in between doing his baking?"

"Hey wait a minute," exclaimed McMary. "Even I didn't know anything about Costas Delupas and drugs, and I've been here over 20 years. How would The Viscount know this? And he had been here only a few days when we went into the store. He didn't even know where the store was until I took him there."

"Come on lady, it doesn't take that long to find drug dealers in this town. All you have to do is ask around."

"Let me tell you, The Viscount is a big drinker but he is definitely not a druggy. He disdains even the thought of that. Where he comes from drugs are never an issue."

"Well by the way The Viscount, just where are you from? Could it be some distant planet in the Milky Way?"

"He is from the Isle of Goda, about 32 miles off the coast of Suriname in South America."

"Look, luscious, I would appreciate it if you didn't answer for this suspect."

"Wait a minute, why on earth is he a suspect? A suspect for what?"

"Lookie here, babe, we've got a murder on our hands and possible other murders, or at least two missing people, maybe more, and we are looking at anyone who is the least bit mysterious, especially newcomers," growled Cosmass.

"Why do you decide a person is a suspect just because he is new here or a little different from the norm?" asked McMary. "That is unfair and uncivilized. The Viscount has done nothing wrong. The only thing he has done is run into that balloon arch at PrideFest. And that was a total accident, since he was looking back to see where I was. And those charges were dropped."

While the Sergeant and McMary were going at it, The Viscount wore a placid visage. He was staring at her cleavage.

"OK, let me go in another direction. How well do either of you know a man named Robert Cleverly, whose real name is Stephen Speciel and who has a long record for killing prize hogs, a serial killer of prize hogs? I don't mean some of the hogs who walk around here," Cosmass said with a chuckle. "Real hogs back in Idaho."

"What has he got to do with us?" asked McMary, nonchalantly pulling away The Viscount's hand from her thigh.

"Haven't you met him? I bet you did."

"We did meet him briefly at Taste of Bulgaria. He was arguing with Costas when we came in. He is a tall, thin man with a sort of fake aristocratic manner."

"What were they arguing about?" asked Cosmass.

"Actually, I think it would be more accurate to say Costas Delupas was yelling at Cleverly. Costas was tough on people he didn't like, and I could tell he didn't like that man. In fact, he told the guy to get out of his store before he threw him out. It was kind of nasty," said McMary.

"So, are you telling me that was the only time you encountered Cleverly?"

"Yes, and we barely recognize his name," said McMary as The Viscount's head was now resting on her left chest. "It was a fleeting moment that we met him, sort of as he was leaving the store."

"Well, could you or your paramour here, tell us why he was the guy who got The Viscount out of jail yesterday? It sounds to me that he knew The Viscount a lot better than you say. Why would Cleverly care about The Viscount, after only a one-time chance meeting?"

"I have no idea. By the time my friends and I got to the jail, The Viscount already was out. He had returned home."

"I find it very odd that a guy you hardly know goes to the trouble of getting The Viscount out of jail, of getting the signatures of 10 or 12 people, all agreeing to a statement of his undeniable innocence. Something smells here, and its more than this guppy you call The Viscount."

At this time, The Viscount was fully reposing in a fetal position on McMary Marimba.

❃

Later that day, the police officers tracked down Robert Cleverly at his house on Windsor Lane, just behind "The Alligator and The Mermaid" inn on Truman Avenue. He had been staying at the inn initially but couldn't afford this "inn of inns" in the city with more inns than any other per capita in the world. After he got out of the hospital after the severe beating he endured at the hands of the bikers outside the Bottle Cap Lounge, he snatched a small rental unit at the house on Windsor Lane.

"All right, we know all about you, Cleverly, or shall we call you Stephen Speciel. My partner here, Officer Sidelitch, Officer Arrow Sidelitch to be complete, would like to know a few things, among them, did you know the guys who beat you up?"

"Oh, no, never saw them before."

"Well, then, tell us why they would come into a bar, play a little pool, and then suddenly decide to beat the living shit out of you."

"I don't know. I don't know. And where the hell were you guys when I was in the hospital. Nobody bothered to investigate anything then, and I was there for six days."

"Listen smart orifice, we could have the whole department out there everyday investigating cases where people were beat up. Usually, the people who were beat up brought it upon themselves. How do you like that refrain, orifice?"

"Well, I'd like to know why am I so important to you now," returned Cleverly.

"Well first of all, shithead – by the way you really do look like a shithead with that one eyeball hanging out and maybe you should get some dentures too and maybe a new ear – we'd like to know why the hell you would round up a bunch of people and have them sign a statement to get that loonybird out of jail. In common language, what's in it for you?"

"Look, I was just trying to help this poor guy who fell off his bike. There were a bunch of people there who saw what happened and suddenly about six of your squad cars were on the guy and I just thought it was unfair.

"I was standing there talking with two girls I met – Shallaha and Charla, two raging dykes if I ever saw them – and this guy runs into the arch of balloons. He was riding a tall unicycle and just toppled into the arbor, and he brushed a lit cigar into one of the balloons and then a bunch of other balloons burst and the next thing was the whole damned thing caught fire. We all thought it was pretty funny, except, shall I say you cops and a few of the PrideFest organizers.

"It was a simple accident. I had been standing right by the arbor. Everyone knew it was an accident. I got a written statement and the signatures of ten other people who saw what happened. He was just looking back for his girlfriend when he hit the arbor. How can you arrest a guy like that? It was only a mistake. He meant no harm. You guys are really too much."

"I'd advise you to watch your mouth with Sergeant Cosmass," intertwined Officer Arrow Sidelitch, only five-eight and as thin as a boat pole. "He's not going to take any crap from you."

"Crap, you silly ass. I'm the one who got beat up and no one cares. Then I try to be a Good Samaritan and you act like I'm under investigation."

"You are, and now let me read you your rights as Officer Sidelitch puts the cuffs on you," chortled Sergeant Cosmass.

❋

CHAPTER TWENTY-ONE

Let Them Eat Cake

WHILE THE COAST GUARD, the drugs and firearms enforcement agents, the state law enforcement arm, the FBI, the Monroe County Sheriff's Deputies, and the Key West police continued their search for Johnny Gordon and Heidi Hamm, the couple were actually out having a good time in Boca Raton. Their friend, Zero Belinsky, the one-armed midget plumber, meanwhile, rested in confinement as the lead suspect in the death of Costas Delupas and more certainly the disappearance of Gordon and Hamm.

Yes, the couple were in Boca at the Boca Beach & Tennis Club, about as swank as it gets.

"Bet you never thought we'd do this, did you Johnny?" Heidi said as they peered out the window by the balcony, overlooking the Atlantic. "So ya finally caught me, and you never thought you would, did ya Johnny?"

Johnny just nodded. He was more taciturn than usual after all the Pabst Blue Ribbons of the previous night and this morning and perhaps second-guessing what he had just done.

"Come on Mississippi Mud, what ya got to say for yourself?"

"I'm just trying to figure how all this happened so fast," said Johnny. "One day you're here, next day you're somewhere else, Heidi. I've just never been able to keep up with you or figure you out."

With that, Heidi gave Johnny a big wet kiss on the lips.

This afternoon, they were having some wedding cake in their suite, the last cake, in fact, baked by the late Costas Delupas.

All and all, Johnny Gordon was in bliss. Well, as blissful as he can be. He had never been in a hotel like this and he never had thought Heidi would settle down with him. In fact she did. Just the day before they had run into a former priest, who was sitting near them at the club's Magic Bar, and he had agreed to marry them right there at the bar. His youthful companion served as best man and a waitress was the matron of honor. Everyone toasted with martinis up, except for Johnny, who had his usual Pabst Blue Ribbon.

Why redneck Johnny would ever agree to go to an exclusive resort like the Boca is anybody's guess. It must have been Heidi's idea. But nonetheless they hopped on Heidi's 1999 Harley Fat Boy and bounded up Route 1 through the Keys and on to Boca, where they took a suite on the beach side of the resort.

They had no idea that their disappearance several days earlier had law enforcement authorities in a dither about where they were. They had no idea that their little buddy Zero Belinsky was in the Monroe County Detention Center, charged with the murder of Costas Delupas and the suspected foul play that may have befallen them.

Johnny couldn't believe Heidi agreed to get married, but then he thought, defeatist that he is, she could divorce him just as quickly. Whatever her whims of the moment were the whims that suited her. Right now, Johnny was the beneficiary.

He figured that when this was over, he might take his ketch and move on to Costa Rica, where land was cheap and he could carry on his fishing and machinist careers in a quieter way. Key West had been getting to him. Maybe find a Costa Rican girl who would treat him like a king, not in the flighty, unpredictable way Heidi did.

In fact, he noted that during their "honeymoon" she had been making eyes at some high-roller golfers who had been at the Magic Bar at the Boca. He furtively noted that at that point they had been married for less than 24 hours, when her glances turned away from him and to the middle-aged guys who obviously were dripping money. The guys thought that she was just a girlfriend or an acquaintance of Johnny's, since she wasn't wearing a wedding band. The marriage happened so quickly that they hadn't had time to get any rings.

Next thing, the guys were sending her drinks, but not to Johnny, which, of course, made Johnny feel like the red neck loser he truly was. Meanwhile, the flirtatious Heidi kept batting those dark eyelashes. She knew how to use every inch of her body to gain attention and then some.

Not long later, one of the guys came over from the other side of the big rectangular bar and started putting the squeeze on Heidi. He positioned himself right between Johnny and Heidi, with his butt right up against Johnny's right shoulder. He never acknowledged Johnny, although the guy knew Johnny had been with Heidi, though he didn't know that they were married. They had run over to their suite right after the marriage and proceeded to consummate it and then fled right back to the bar for more drinks.

The guy was engaged in a rip roaring conversation with Heidi, who never once bothered to introduce Johnny, who looked about as out of place at the Boca as anyone could be. He looked like the rube from the small town near Biloxi that he was.

Now the guy was kissing the base of Heidi's neck, slurping up to her left ear, tongue darting in and out. Heidi never refused his advances. Never said she had just gotten married to the man on the stool to the left.

Her yellow belly shirt burst in many bouncy directions as the man's advances got her going. The man couldn't get over her body. Everything was perfecto. Incredible ballet dancer-like legs. Great strawberry blonde hair that was today pinned up in two pigtails. Kind of what Doris Day looked like in those early 1950s color movies. What a butt, the guy thought. This broad is definitely available, he thought.

That was the last thought he had before they rushed him to the hospital bleeding to death.

Johnny had had all that he could take, pulled out a seven-inch fishing knife that he always carried strapped to his body underneath his shirt. Never uttered a word.

He took one plunge of the knife that penetrated one of the guy's lungs and a vital artery. This guy would be a goner because of the damage inflicted. There were no more comments or slurping from him, though he did emit a gurgling sound as he proceeded to drown in his own blood.

It happened so fast that Heidi didn't realize what occurred. She first thought that the guy had had a heart attack or a stroke or just passed out. Until she saw all the blood, and saw Johnny holding his prized possession, the fishing knife.

In the milliseconds that ensued, Johnny had pulled his knife out of the guy and proceeded to slit his own throat from end to end. This was not a stable guy. As he himself proceeded to die right there at the bar, he bent over and put his arms down with his head on them and wept until his last breath was drawn. He gurgled, too.

The Boca police descended upon the Magic Bar within minutes and sent the two wounded or dead men away in EMS vans. And they took Heidi into the station for questioning, thinking she had had something to do with this carnage. And, of course, we all know she did.

CHAPTER TWENTY-TWO

Heidi Takes On Some Fellow Bikers

IT WASN'T LONG BEFORE Heidi was released from questioning by the Boca Raton police and she was back on Route U.S. 1 heading toward Key West. She was now a widow, only two days after she was married.

She wasn't too happy that the police were trying to infer that she might be a hooker. Sometimes these girls slip into the Magic Bar. But, quickly, when she produced evidence that she was staying at the hotel they began to assume that she was just a guest. They thought her marriage to Johnny Gordon was bogus though. She could produce no paper, and they knew the ex-priest who married them as a con artist, pedophiliac, hemophiliac and crossdresser who would do anything for money to buy drinks.

They asked her if she was interested in taking care of Johnny's remains, sending them somewhere. She could not think of where though. She didn't know his home address in Opley, Mississippi, or that there were any remaining relatives there. She asked the cops to keep him on cool to see if somebody in Key West would take him and make funeral arrangements. Maybe Zero Belinsky she thought, not knowing that he was in jail and couldn't do a thing about it at the moment.

Oh well, she thought, time to head back to K.W. She had some remorse for what had happened to Johnny but not much. She is the type of person that essentially doesn't always know her impact on things but she does know how to get her way with men. Heidi always thought Johnny was mentally unstable. To suddenly kill a man with a big knife and then take that knife to himself would indicate this notion was so, she thought.

At Marathon Key, she ran into a couple of other bikers and decided to ride down to Key West with them. One guy's name was Weasel Windsiege and the other, a guy of Cuban descent, had the name of Hreben Cruiz.

They both appeared to be in their mid to late 30s. They would look menacing to most people, but not to Heidi Hamm.

She had stopped at the Halfway Bar to get something to eat and a couple of beers. The two guys spotted her and started up a chat. She said she was from Key West, they said they were from Miami.

"So what's a girl like you driving up and down the highway by yourself?" asked Weasel. "A lot of weirdos go up and down this road. You should watch yourself."

"Oh, I do it all the time," said Heidi. "I'm not afraid. Sometimes I go with somebody and sometimes I don't."

"Well, a beaut like you ought to be careful," Weasel said with a frown. "You might run into horny guys like us."

Hreben Cruiz, darkly Cuban and a thin and gangly man with one piercing dark eye and the other missing, or at least there was no iris, just a filmy, milky tissue, then spoke up, "Let us escort you back to Key West. The sun's going down. We'll stop at some bars along the way and have us a friggin' good time, babe."

"Why not?" said the bride/widow. "Let's have us some fun!"

Seated at another table in the cozy little place were Ted Obretta and Sheriff's Deputy Lovie Jones, a shear accident. Lovie knew Obretta was planning to leave Key West the next day and said, "Why don't we pick up a bike for you and we'll go up the keys a bit and see some spots you wouldn't know about? In fact, why don't we let me ride the rental and you can take my Suzuki 550 and zip around, bro? I appreciate your help on the Delupas case."

So the guys took a trip northward and coincidentally ended up at the Halfway Bar. Lovie, the ultimate investigator, tapped Ted on the hand and nodded over to the table where the grizzly bikers had now been sitting with Heidi Hamm. Ex-Philly detective Ted would not have known Heidi from anyone else, but he followed Deputy Jones' lead and made no overt movements in Heidi's direction. "That's Heidi Hamm," whispered Deputy Jones. "That's the one who disappeared with Johnny Gordon after they found Costas Delupas dead."

"What do you want to do, go over and talk to them?" as Obretta.

"Hell no, nothing. Let's just observe them, that's all."

"Those are the guys I saw at the Schooner Wharf a couple of days ago. They look suspicious to me, like drug runners."

"Everyone looks suspicious to you," said Jones with a chuckle. "Next thing you're going to think I'm implicated in the Delupas murder. And you know, Johnny Gordon is still missing. Maybe I'm involved with that too, but not Heidi Hamm, because that little bitch is right here before us, front and center."

"I wonder about Johnny Gordon and whether he and Heidi may have had something to do with the Delupas killing," said Ted Obretta. "They disappeared right after his body was found. "I'd like to talk with both of them."

"Not now, bro, not now," responded Lovie Jones. "We're in an observational state of mind. Let's just follow them and see where they go. Like Ted Obretta, Deputy Jones looked like just another tourist on his rental Yamaha, with the little Key West Cycle sign on it. The people they were following would probably never guess that they were in law enforcement; well at least one of them still was.

"You know, I have to ask you, bro, what in hell are you spending so much time volunteering on this investigation when you could be in the beer halls and on the piers of Key West getting' some suds and some sun on your little vacation here?"

"I don't know, but for some reason I feel close to this case," said the ex detective. "I feel as though I have run up against or at least near the people or person who killed Costas Delupas, and the officer in me just wants to figure this out."

"Well, let me tell you, bro, you can mess around with me 'cause I'm an older deputy and I like you, but you start foolin' with some of the younger guys in the Sheriff's Office or the Key West police or, my God, the feds, and you will be hung by your petard for obstructing justice. We have enough competition amongst ourselves that we don't need any gumshoes from the north buttin' in. Kapeesh?"

Jones and Obretta followed Heidi Hamm and her new biker friends all the way into Key West, right to the Bull & the Whistle on Duval. They went up to the second floor and sat on the balcony watching the parade of Key West visitors below.

Ted Obretta and Lovie Jones meanwhile hunkered down at a little open bar across the street where they would continue to observe the trio.

Lovie was wondering what the hell happened to Johnny Gordon. He soon found out.

He had called the Sheriff's Office to check for messages, and a deputy there informed him that Johnny Gordon was found dead in Boca Raton. He had killed a man in an upscale bar at an upper-crust hotel there and then, apparently, killed himself. Deputy Jones learned that Heidi Hamm was questioned in the incident and later released.

"This blonde bombshell went from getting married to being widowed in less than 48 hours, and didn't seem to be concerned about shipping her husband's body any place special," said Lovie Jones to Ted Obretta. "But the officers in Boca, when they found out we had Johnny Gordon and Heidi Hamm on our missing persons' report, took a look at the suite they had been staying in and discovered a wedding cake that was in a box from Taste of Bulgaria, Costas Delupas's bakery. What do you think about that? Costas always put the date and time his cakes were finished on the box and as far as our deputies can conclude, that was the last cake he baked the day he was found floating in the mangroves. Woooooiieeee! I think we are on to something here, bro.

"We can't talk to poor Johnny but we can talk to that broad across the street. I'm going to send some deputies over to the Whistle and bring her in for questioning," said Deputy Jones. "This is clearly our case, and not the case of the Key West police because we started observing her in Marathon, half way up Monroe County.

"She and Johnny were probably the last people to be in Costas Delupas's store that day. They were going on a trip up the coast and maybe they decided to buy more than just a wedding cake. Whadya think, Ted?"

"Yeah, I think you're on to something. I'd question those bikers too," Ted said, not knowing Heidi had just met the bikers several hours earlier.

To Ted, half the people in Key West were under suspicion.

❈

CHAPTER TWENTY-THREE

Heidi Slips Away

HEIDI HAD BEEN LOOKING down at the deputy and the ex detective from the balcony of the Bull & Whistle. She seemed to think that the two guys at the bar across the street were cops, or undercover agents, and her fear was that they were observing her with Weasel Windsiege and Hreben Cruiz, the two bikers who picked her up in Marathon. She decided to slip out to the girl's room on the second floor and then down the back steps of the bar.

Ted Obretta, the man who is suspicious of all souls, should have been paying better attention, as Deputy Lovie Jones went to the back of the bar to call his office. No, Ted was looking at some other people on Duval, thinking he had seen them before during one of his details a couple of days earlier. He was looking over his notes, trying to recall their faces. Meanwhile, Heidi slipped away.

Well, sort of.

Instead of going down the steep back stairs and heading south down Caroline Street and over to Whitehead, where she thought she'd have a beer at the Green Parrot, she decided to go up the stairs to the Garden of Eden. At night one of the favorite activities there is full-length body painting. This was one of Heidi's kicks and she decided to have the complete treatment, even coloring her strawberry hair black. By the time this was done, no one would have recognized Heidi Hamm, hideously colored from toe to ta-tas and about the neck and head. She looked strange, but not for Key West. Then she went down to the Parrot on the corner of Whitehead and Southard and proceeded to have a good time with old friends there and meet some new ones.

When the deputies arrived at the Whistle they didn't find Heidi but only the two bikers whom they took in for questioning, noting that they had been seen with Heidi Hamm over the past several hours. The deputies wanted to talk with Heidi but she would be no where to be found and not that identifiable.

Deputy Lovie Jones and Ted Obretta went to the Sheriff's offices to observe the questioning.

"These are the same guys that I saw a few nights ago at the Schooner Wharf," said Obretta. "One of them wanted to pick a fight with a macaw and his owner, an older gentleman from Ubi, you know that guy who has been on TV so much for saving his country from people who were trying to take it over."

"He comes here a lot, to get away. One time he brought the former President of the United States, Hanford Simpson, with him. The old guy loves Key West, stays at a suite upstairs at the Pier House," said Deputy Jones.

"Anyway, the other night I thought these guys were going to bust this Premier Ubi Ubi guy in the chops and snap his bird's neck," said Obretta. "I had to step in. I didn't realize they were the same guys as the ones the deputies just took in."

"So what do you guys have to do with Heidi Hamm?" asked one of the deputies, Turgell Sod.

"Nothing," said Weasel. "We just met her at the Halfway Bar in Marathon and rode down to Key West with her. What's wrong with that?"

"Do you know that she may be under suspicion in the murder of Costas Delupas?" asked the deputy.

"How would I know that?" returned Weasel. "I didn't even know there was a murder in Key West until a couple of days ago. We've been up in Miami for the past week."

"We've been told the Key West police have a man named Richard Cleverly in custody. Did you ever hear of him?" asked Deputy Sod. "He was beat to a pulp outside the Bottle Cap bar about a week ago by two bikers. And the descriptions we've been given by the police witnesses are unquestionably similar to yours and your friend here. Have you anything to say about this?"

"Well, we don't think you can match the time we were in Key West with the time you say that Cleverly guy was beat Up. I keep telling you we were in Miami for the past week," said Weasel.

"Do you know Zero Belinsky?"

"Never heard of him," responded Weasel.

"Are you sure you never heard of him?"

"Never."

"Well, he knows who you guys are. And he tells us that you guys might have killed Costas Delupas, said Deputy Sod."

"Hey, that guy was poisoned, man," said Weasel. "If we were going to do someone, we would do him with something a lot stronger than rat poison."

"Well, it's interesting that you know about the rat poison. That was only reported in *The Key West Citizen* three days ago, and I'm sure it never made The Miami Herald," said Deputy Sod, as Deputy Jones and Ted Obretta looked on through a one-way window, with the 3-8 one-armed midget plumber Zero Belinsky sitting nearby, guarded by another deputy.

Zero was whimpering. He had just heard of Johnny Gordon's death up in Boca.

Ted turned to Sheriff's Deputy Lovie Jones and said, "We have too many suspects and not enough motives to the Delupas murder."

And with that, another deputy interrupted with the message that the Key West police have just reported that The Pelican, also known as Ramsey Fletcher, the gay prince of Key West parties, had been found dead in his bed in his house on Mickens Lane. He had been garrotted to death or perhaps smothered with a big red MacIntosh apple or both. When police found him he looked like a chubby, overstuffed pig, lying supine in one of his jivey kimonos.

CHAPTER TWENTY-FOUR

How Things Went Afoul At Ol' Jose Marti's Place

LaTeDa is one of the finest gathering places for heteros and gays in all of Key West. Good food, good entertainment and fine booze. Lots of gossip too.

The Pelican had been there the night of his death, telling bountiful stories, most of which were untrue but colorful nonetheless. Located at 1125 Duval, it is the former home of Jose Marti, long considered to be the George Washington of Cuba. LaTeDa was shortened from its original name, La Terraza de Marti, the name the Cuban poet-patriot gave it well over a century ago. At the time Key West was the wealthiest city in America what with its shipping, sponging, commercial fishing, shipwrecking and, especially, cigar-making industries flourishing.

Today, and for the past number of years, LaTeDa is a place of great cross-dresser shows in the upstairs theater. The shows have various headliners and a number of lesser lights, but most of the talent is worth going back to see, stars such as Randy Roberts or one of the older hosts, MaJon, aka David Felstein. It is a place remindful of Toulouse Lautrec's Moulin Rouge era up in the Montmartre section of Paris. And, always, a great place to people watch.

The Pelican was sitting at the inside bar (there is a terrific outside bar too, on the patio), talking with Gary Bluett and Artie Pepico. As usual The Pelican was in a braggadocios mood, telling the boys about his extensive jewelry collection, much of it from the American southwest, where he used to reside. Then he was off talking about his hand pottery collection, his pewter castings and his extensive Raymond Weil watch collection. "I'd take Raymond Weil over Rolex anytime… it goes up in value significantly." And, lastly, he talked about the diamonds he inherited from his mother and also the art hanging on the wall of Conch bungalow on Mickens Lane.

"You usually have so many people at your parties that we hardly notice all this," said Gary.

"Oh, my yes, I should show you boys some of the stuff I have hidden away; it's worth several fortunes," returned The Pelican.

Why he would talk so openly about his treasures is anybody's guess, but then Key West is an essentially safe community where people often don't lock their doors. And it was his way to talk, talk, talk about himself, the people he knew and his possessions.

"I was a dear friend of Pinochet, the great leader of Chile (some other people would call him an anti-Marxist dictator), and President Hanover Simpson, when he was governor of Texas... he visits me whenever he comes to Key West... and Hanover's good friend Premier Ubi Ubi of Ubi... I knew Rock Hudson well in Bel Air... and Theodore Bikel when I was in New York... and when I was a young lad, I used to read poetry to Mao Tse Tung," The Pelican would ramble in strange sequences.

"I used to play bridge with Tennessee Williams and Parcheesi with Picasso when he visited here... and Salvador Dali, we played horseshoes often, and I was good friends with Harriet Nelson of the Nelson family and her sons Rick and Dave. Didn't know Ozzie that well. Toscanini taught me some tricks on how to play the fiddle when I had my flat on East 63rd in Manhattan and Pola Negri visited there as well. And, oh, Durwood Kirby, we were such nice friends."

For a guy nearing seventy or past seventy, The Pelican had energy – especially when talking about himself.

He had a high-pitched voice that somehow tweaked different areas of a room. In other words, you could usually tell The Pelican was there, without even seeing him. And then when you saw him, the whole package came together, gaudy and somewhat seedy, but also with some good taste thrown in.

The Pelican was voted Queen Mother of Key West

during PrideFest a few years ago. He especially liked to yak it up with his fellow Queen Mothers when they would gather for tea at LaTeDa. This was like a fraternity, or sorority, if you will. Their motto was: "Once a Queen Mother always a Queen Mother!"

But the brutish question of the moment was who would have killed The Pelican and why.

All his possessions seemed to be in place when the police discovered the crime the next morning. A neighbor had notified them when she found the door to his home wide open at 7 a.m. and the stereo blasting full force, with the smells of a potroast in the oven. The Pelican was never known to get up before 10 or 11 a.m.

So the police walked in and found him on his cantilevered canopy bed with the Queen Mother's shield on the headboard. "He is dead as a bottomfeeder fish lying sideways on the beach," said one of the officers.

The Pelican's eyes were bulging out from the garrotte or from the fulsome MacIntosh apple that had been pushed halfway into his mouth. One of the other officers said, "He looks ready for roasting."

So that was the end of The Pelican, after more than 30 years of of Cayo Hueso partying. The Pelican will undoubtedly be talked about for many years more and still be part of the town's colorful lore.

That night LaTeDa was of course abuzz with the murder of The Pelican. Gary Bluett and Artie Pepico were at their usual seats at the inside bar telling everyone in sight that they had just been sitting with The Pelican the night before.

And, of course, seated at a high table and chair past the bar was Ted Obretta, who heard by the Key West grapevine that The Pelican had spent his last night at LaTeDa, before perhaps going to the much enjoyed late night private parties somewhere else.

Ted was sitting there, smoking a Griffin robusto and drinking a mojito and watching and listening. Because of the large crowd, Gary and Artie were oblivious to his presence.

Ted was most confused. There were so many possible suspects in the Delupas case and now this murder. Would that be it or would there be more? He thought the latter.

So he decided to extend his vacation a few days more. When he got back to their rented house in the Truman Annex, two of his buddies were packing to go home.

Zemblon Yurcocitch, the podiatrist from Buffalo, said, "A bunch of stinky feet – and some good green cash – are waiting for me." Charlie York, ever the Ivy-Leaguer with the slicked-back blond hair, had to return to his clients in Philadelphia, and ribbingly said to Ted, "Nice to have you on this trip, Obretta; can't wait for our next one. Where would you like to go next time, Afghanistan? You could route out the dirty dogs from al Qaeda and the Taliban, while we chase the horny Afghani girls who are seeking to fulfill their liberation.

"Where the hell you been all week?" Charlie continued. "I hope whatever you've been doing was as enjoyable as it was for us. We missed you at Louie's Backyard last night and Café des Artistes this evening. You missed all that great food; the snook and the duck were outstanding. Had plenty of Stonestreet merlot at both places. You are really something, Ted."

One of the others from the group of four wouldn't be returning just yet either. Whitlow Wyatt had some "unfinished business" with Pansy Riviera, and he got her to stay a few days more. He also wondered about Ted.

"Let me tell you something, Whit, I couldn't help myself with this Delupas case, the disappearance of Johnny Gordon and Heidi Hamm and now the murder of The Pelican, who's also known as Ramsey Fletcher," said Ted. "On top of that, this guy Robert Cleverly gets the shit beat out of him by two bikers for apparently no reason, but I think there is a reason. Then Johnny Gordon turns up in Boca, knifes some guy and then kills himself and, get this, his girlfriend Heidi is observed with two bikers, shortly after Johnny died. Then there is this mysterious guy who calls himself The Viscount and says he comes from the Isle of Goda, a place no one has ever heard of.

"That's not to say anything about Shamir O'Neill, who discovered the head of Costas Delupas in the mangroves. He turned it in several days after the body was found. The Coast Guard, the federal drug agents, the Monroe County game warden and the immigration officials have been watching him. Or what about Zero Belinsky, the one-armed midget plumber who is being held in Costas Delupas's death?

"These are questions that must be answered. I can't help but getting involved with this mystery. You would, too, if you had spent as much time on the force as I have. I may be retired but my mind is still inquisitive."

"You need to chill, Ted. You really need to chill," said Charlie.

❇

CHAPTER TWENTY-FIVE

More Intrigue At The Bottom Of Duval

THE VISCOUNT AND McMary were enjoying cocktails at One Duval in The Pier House. They were enjoying a fine jazz stylist on the piano and striking up a conversation with a couple who were deeply into each other, Whitlow Wyatt and Pansy Riviera.

On the other side of The Viscount and McMary were those treasure warriors from the Williamsburg neighborhood of Brooklyn, New York, but residents of Key West now for a good 25 years, Morky Golub and Seamus Fine. With them was their friend, Rabbi Otto Blintz, who was enjoying an extra, extra dry Beefeater martini, up, with two kosher olives he had brought with him in the pocket of his black wool jacket.

Everybody was having a good time and chatting it up with one another.

Of course, the conversation drifted into the

Delupas case and the discovery of the murder of The Pelican.

"I theeenk it twas probably someone wee alla know," said the rabbi. "I juss hope dere von't bee more. It is scaring everybody aroun' here."

"The guy that is in custody for the Delupas murder is a good friend of ours who wouldn't hurt a flea," commented Morky.

"I think they have him in jail more because he knows or knew Johnny Gordon and Heidi Hamm well," added Seamus Fine. "The police just assumed there might be some connection with the Delupas killing. They should really let our friend Zero Belinksy go because the evidence is very circumstantial and the only support was that he was the last guy to see Johnny and Heidi before they disappeared. Now Johnny is accounted for – dead by his own hand – and Heidi is back in captivity. I just don't see what the hell they have with Zero and Delupas. Zero doesn't do drugs and he wasn't that much of a fan of baked goods. The only thing he might have had against Delupas is that the baker beat him twice in the arm wrestling part of the Hemingway Days competition. Zero was so mad then that with his one arm he gave Delupas a well-placed jolt to the balls after the arm wrestling. I don't think Zero held any grudges after that."

Meanwhile, Pansy and Whitlow were loving it up down the right side of the splendiferous bar, a bar that looked like it was a northern one. Definitely not a Florida one.

"I'm so happy we could spend these extra days in Key West after all that witness-giving we had to do this past week," said Whit Wyatt.

"I just wonder when we'll get to see each other again," responded Pansy. "Kato, Iowa, is a long way from Buffalo, New York."

"Well, maybe I can get you to move to Buffalo," said Whitlow. "We have plenty of schools for you to teach at, plus it's a stone's throw from Toronto and only 60 miles north of Ellicottville, New York, where there's some great skiing."

"Let's just enjoy our time here and we can think about the other stuff later," said Pansy.

"Whe're you staying in Key West?" asked McMary.

"I was in the Truman Annex and then moved over to The Gardens on Simonton with Pansy here," answered Whitlow. "It's a beautiful inn with about 17 rooms. It's like living inside an arboretum or a botanical garden. Really quaint and warm."

"We live at the corner of Duval and United on the eastern side of the island," McMary responded with a broad smile showing her perfect white teeth.

"This here is my friend, The Viscount, who is from

the Isle of Goda but is now making Key West his second home."

"So good to meet you this lovely day," said The Viscount, turning to his right to greet the couple.

"I've heard of you," said Morky Golub from the other side of the bar. "You have become quite the talk of the town. How do you like riding your tall unicycle around town? How high is it anyway? Every time I think I've seen everything in Key West, I see something odder yet."

"It's nine feet high tall, so that puts me at least 12-feet off the ground. I like riding around up there. In fact, back home I've got a 20-foot unicycle, which I would have taken with me, but I couldn't get it in my sailing egg," said The Viscount.

"I've some trouble here getting entangled in the overhead wires and the other day I inadvertently knocked down the balloon arbor at PrideFest and caused it to catch fire with my cigar," The Viscount continued.

"We have read about your exploits in *The Citizen* and the *Solares Hill* newspaper. I think you were even in *Key West, The Newspaper,* and *Celebrate,* the gay newspaper. You are becoming a real celebrity around here," mentioned Seamus.

The Viscount nodded somewhat embarrassingly. McMary put her arm around his shoulder and ruffled with one of his epaulets. "You are exactly what Key West is all about, love. You can be your own self around here without the condemnation of anyone. You are indicative of our belief that we are one human family."

"Thank you so much, McMary. But if I hadn't met you on the first day I would have just stood out as a weird one. With you, I have some credibility. Thank you so much, honeybuns."

The various people at the bar continued to exchange pleasantries as the sun came down on the Gulf of Mexico, just outside. They did so, until another customer came into the bar, and asked, "Did you hear? Someone else has been found murdered, Gary Bluett, the interior furnishings designer."

The patron said he was down by the Key West police station on Angela when they brought in the suspect, Bluett's roommate, Artie Pepico. "The guy was crying and sobbing, claiming he had nothing to do with the murder, that he didn't know what he was going to do now that his friend had suddenly died."

Just a few minutes later, Ted Obretta arrived at the bar and was transfixed by the latest criminal development.

He thought he'd get involved in the conversation at the bar. Ted knew McMary and The Viscount and certainly had been acquainted with Gary Bluett during the past week. Maybe some other people there could help with more information. He sat on the other side of Rabbi

Blintz, Morky and Seamus, thinking he'd like to get to know them as well. They looked suspicious to Ted. He had agreed to meet them for drinks after they had paid him a surprise visit at his rental home in the Annex.

Ted knew the couple – his friend Whitlow Wyatt and Wyatt's latest squeeze, Pansy Riviera – sitting at the other end of the bar, were the ones who discovered the be-headed corpse of Costas Delupas earlier in the week. He wanted to connect the dots in these murders; he figured they all were related. But he still was befuddled as to what the motives could be.

Ted, acting as the touron inquisitor, asked out loud so the whole group could hear him, "Does anybody think that these three people who were killed were connected in any way? Does anybody think they knew each other well?

"I do, I do," said Rabbi Blintz.

"How can you say that Otto?" asked Morky. "Do you think you really knew these people? "I bet you never even met The Pelican. I really don't think you knew Gary Bluett, did you? The one you probably knew the best was Costas Delupas."

"It is juss my rabbinical intuition. Juss that. I've beeen in za beeziness for too many years not to have intuition."

"Well, now, my dear friend, you think you are a detective," parried Seamus.

With that, The Viscount opined, "Hey, that guy next to you is a real detective from Philadelphia.

Ted Obretta answered, "Yeah, well I used to be a detective, but I've been retired a few years. Just here on vacation." Obretta preferred to act undercover and didn't want to breech his real interest in the crimes.

"Oy, vey," said the rabbi. "Vat eeze happening een paradise? Vat eeze happening?"

"Frankly," said Ted, "I agree with the rabbi here. If these things seem to happen in a series, it is often the case that they are related. It could involve more than one killer or perhaps just one." **Ted could have slapped himself for showing a card or two;** he had always been trained – and he had trained other detectives – to play it close to the vest. For all he knew, he could be sitting with one or more of the murderers. Why give them any help?

❂

After having a couple of drinks at One Duval, the group, all of them, decided to walk over to the American Bar on Front Street, not far away. Like One Duval, the American Bar bespeaks something you'd see in New York City or Chicago, more than a Key West place. The only thing betraying Key West was that at the American, you can sit outside at a long, sophisticated bar, listen to some good live Latin or mainstream jazz music, and do so under roof but in the open air.

It was dark now, and this strangely assembled group of people seemed to be enjoying themselves. Ted, of course, turned the occasion into another police detail.

He was growing ever more suspicious of the rabbi and his two friends, Morky and Seamus, even though they continued to buy him drinks and were Key West friendly toward him.

The conversation continued about the murders. And there was a point when Whitlow and Pansy began talking about their discovery of Delupas's headless body in the submarine slips by the mangroves, up in the waters northwest of Key West. Ted cued into this with both ears. He had not seen much of his buddy from Buffalo most of the week and he never really heard the story directly from the two of them.

He thought that they must know a lot more about the Delupas murder than they might be letting on. He didn't care that the county sheriff's deputies, the Key West police, the state law enforcement officials, the FBI and other authorities had already interrogated them for the better part of two days.

Ted left the group for a few minutes to make a cell call to Deputy Lovie Jones to tell him that he planned the evening talking with this couple and the others. Ted even had some suspicion of Whitlow Wyatt, one of the friends he was vacationing with. But he was more suspicious of Pansy.

❋

"You stupid ass, Obretta," retorted Jones. "These people aren't under investigation for anything. They discovered the body and are simply witnesses."

"I don't know, Lovie, they seem to be holding back to me. They have hardly said a word to the group I'm with. They seem to be holding back."

"Well, maybe that's because all the feds, the Coast Guard, the Navy, the cops and my department screwed them around for two days, when they were supposed to be on vacation," said Jones. "We overdid it. They seem to be swooning after each other, bro. Weren't you ever infatuated with anyone and you really didn't care to talk to anyone else?"

With that comment Ted momentarily thought back to his late wife, Chia, who had left him and then died of sulfuric poisoning looking for the remains of ancient hominid men in Ethiopia. She had left him but Ted still thought of himself as a widower.

"Leave 'em alone, Obretta. I'm beginning to think you could screw up a wet dream," Deputy Jones snarled. "Leave 'em alone, Obretta. They have had enough."

"Well then I have some other observations. I'm also with three guys that know that midget Belinsky guy, and you guys have the little shit in custody at the detention center. Don't you think that they are people we should be looking at?"

"So what!" shouted Deputy Jones. "When is it criminal to be friends with somebody? They are all part of a small Jewish clan in Key West. We've never had any trouble with those guys you mention. We know who they are, because each of them has been out to see Belinsky."

"OK, Lovie, I'm also with McMary Marimba and the guy who calls himself The Viscount. You know The Viscount's already been in custody of the Key West police and McMary's harboring him."

"Look, McMary's been around Key West a good 20 years and more. I can't speak to her boyfriend, don't know enough about him, but, man, you outta let go, Obretta. You are really pissing up a rope this time. Why don't you take some Valium and go back on the vacation you were supposed to have? I can't believe you are even suspicious of your friend from Buffalo."

"He was missing from our group of four guys for most of the week. I don't know what that girl, Pansy, may have put him up to," said Ted.

"What about you, bro? Haven't you been missing even more? I bet you hardly spent any time with your colleagues because your big ass Italian nose had to get involved with all this shit. Don't you know what the word retired means? You're retired, you're on vacation and you're adding to the confusion of an already confounding series of murders."

With that, Ted went back to the group of revelers to seek more answers to his questions, never offering to pay for a drink.

❇

CHAPTER TWENTY-SIX

Another Day, Another Murder

TED OBRETTA APPARENTLY has no shame. He continued talking that night with The Viscount and McMary Marimba, the couple just several days earlier he had been watching copulate on top of a three-decker tomb site at the old cemetery, where some people had been resting peacefully for better than 150 years. They did not know he had been the fellow who had been arrested and briefly held in custody for voyeurism.

Ted is not above the law, he just thinks it his banner to uphold it.

"Perhaps, Ted, you'd like to come down to our house to have an after-dinner cordial, perhaps some Dubonet or a Goda Gottcha, the specialty drink of my homeland, the Isle of Goda," blithely suggested The Viscount, after the rest of the group packed it in and went home. Ted, of course, leaped at this suggestion, because he thought that McMary and The Viscount might ask him to stay at their place since it was now well past 2 a.m. They'd have the drinks, go to bed, and he would then be free to scour the house for evidence.

So he went to the house, he had a couple Goda Gottchas, they asked him to stay, they went to bed, and Ted went to work.

This was a big house, on the corner of United and Duval, and he had plenty of exploring to do and he told himself not to be distracted by the sounds McMary and The Viscount were making in the boudoir on the second floor. After they fell asleep, he was convinced that he could thoroughly case the house, even the room they were in.

Moments after their noises of love had stopped, Ted was sure he could mount his investigation. Ted went back to the front porch where the three of them had been enjoying the Goda Gottchas – a cross among a Tequilla Sunrise, a Pisco Sour, a Key Lime martini, with a hint of the suds of a Guiness Stout – and he fell through the floorboards. Termites. It was a loud crash and Ted found himself standing on the ground below.

McMary came rumbling down the second floor staircase and out the front door. She said, "Oh, we've been meaning to fix that," that being the right side of the "L"-shaped porch facing the house. "Ted, let me help you out of there."

"Boy, was that a surprise!" exclaimed Ted. "I was just going out on the porch to have another Gottcha. I wanted one more before I hit the sack, wanted to watch the night-lifers passing by on Duval."

"I hope you aren't hurt," said McMary.

"No, I've had the floor fall from me before when I was an investigating detective, but not literally. Pretty funny. Just a few scrapes."

"We should have told you about this. That's why we always sit on the other side. This house is so rickety. It really needs fixing up, but it has great architecture, great possibilities," said McMary.

"That's all right, just go back to bed. I'm fine; I'll just sit on the swing over there on the left side."

As soon as Ted Obretta was sure the couple above were again soundly asleep he had that last Goda Gottcha and continued perusing the place.

While The Viscount snored and McMary nestled in The Viscount's arms about an hour later, Ted was astonished at what he discovered in the bedroom next to theirs.

It was the body of Shallaha Obbst. Like The Pelican, she had been garroted to death. But instead of stuffing a McIntosh apple in her mouth, as was the case with The Pelican, the killer had forced a long green palm frond down her throat, as extra measure. And like the late Gary Bluett, her left pinky was missing, though another difference in the three murders was that Gary was asphyxiated not with just a normal garrote but instead with a sturdy leather hatband, which had been left on the bedroom floor.

Thoughts were racing through Ted's aching head. 'So many similarities, so many dissimilarities,' he reckoned. And he was willing to bet that the worst was not over.

But back to Shallaha. She was beginning to smell awful.

There were now four murders: Costas Delupas, the baker/small-time drug dealer; The Pelican, the gay blade of Key West couture; Gary Bluett, the interior designer; and now Shallaha Obbst. Three of the victims were gay. Was that a link?

Probably not, because the next morning, Whitlow Wyatt was found dead as well. He was found lying beneath a palm on Simonton Street, a large coconut lying next to his head. Thousands of people around the world die each year from coconuts falling on their heads. But this time the Key West police found foul play. Witnesses spotted someone up in the coconut tree while Whitlow jogged by around 7 a.m. This was near Simonton and Fleming streets. That was not the only thing the witnesses, sitting on their porches or walking by saw. The person in the tree had also thrown the head of Costas Delupas at Whitlow. It is undetermined what actually killed Whitlow Wyatt, the skull of

Delupas with the still flourishing handlebar moustache or the 10-pound coconut.

Whoever was in the tree was able to climb down and jump to the street and run off toward Eaton and on up northward. The perpetrator was of medium height, wore a big straw hat and an orange cape, was hard to define otherwise, and just ran like hell, discarding his or her disguise as he or she went north on Eaton and down one of the alleys.

One of the witnesses was Simon Chuckski who was sitting on the porch of his Conch bungalow with his ravishing girlfriend, Jacquelina El Bartelo.

"We saw what we thought were two coconuts falling out of our tree. Jacquie said, quickly, 'I hope they don't hit that guy!'" said Chuckski. "And all of a sudden, like scud missiles, these two coconuts hit him directly on top of the head, one after the other."

"God you're a knockout!" said Officer Chaz Lakestein, as he started to interview the couple, referring to Jacquie, not Chuckski, who didn't look bad at all, depending on your point of view.

"You married to this guy, you dating him, or are you available, ma'am?" asked Lakestein.

"I don't go out with cops," Jacquie retorted. "And for your information I'm dating Simon, but what does that have to do with the fact that a man on our street was killed by a coconut and a head?"

"Look, lady, don't give me any lip, I'm just trying to do my job," said Lakestein, as an EMS crew put Wyatt in a body bag.

"Have you ever seen the man who was hit by the head and coconut?" continued the officer.

"Never," said Chuckski. "He was jogging down Simonton when it happened. Then we saw this person suddenly scaling down the palm tree and jumping. Everything happened so fast that it seemed like a blur. By the way, whose head was it?"

"We have a pretty good idea it was the head of Costas Delupas, the baker who was murdered last week. He had been decapitated, and the head and his body were in the morgue, chilling, until more of the investigation was completed," answered the officer, now scratching his crotch.

"You mean somebody stole the head from the morgue? How could that happen?" asked Chuckski, reclining on a wicker chair on his front porch.

"We don't know. We didn't even know the head was missing until this incident. We can't keep track of everything, and by the way, that is the responsibility of the Monroe County Sheriff's Office, not us.

"Now tell me about this person who jumped out of the tree. Have you a description?" the officer asked, picking at his right nostril.

"Well, he had kind of a straw musketeer's hat on and a blue jacket with epaulets the color of egg yolks. He originally had an orange cape on but threw it to the ground after he started running toward Eaton Street. He was also wearing short gray pants and black riding boots," mentioned Jacquelina, who looked even more stunning than usual with the early sun peering down on her reddish blonde hair and gorgeous face. "And then he, or it could have been a she it happened so fast, ran down Simonton up Eaton.

"Simon could have caught him but he tripped over the head."

"Yeah, I bolted right out of the front gate and would have been right on that person's butt but I have to trip over the head. I could have caught him."

"Don't feel bad, honey, shit happens," Jacquelina said.

"Yeah, and now we'll probably get sued for the coconut falling out of our tree," concluded Chuckski

"I wouldn't worry about that, sir. I think it is fairly likely that both somewhat spherical objects were thrown at the victim. That's what I'm going to put in my report.

"Let me say, people, it is best you didn't apprehend the suspect. He could have been armed and then we'd be potentially dealing with another murder. We already have five on our hands in the past week," suggested Officer Lakestein."

As they continued to talk, another officer was bagging the head of Costas Delupas as evidence. He threw the coconut in the same sack.

CHAPTER TWENTY-SEVEN

The Police Chase Down
The Viscount

Naturally, the first suspect the Key West police thought of was that visitor from the Isle of Goda, The Viscount.

They went immediately to the house on Duval at United and ran up the front steps like a herd of warthogs.

Ted Obretta greeted them at the door. He had been having breakfast with The Viscount and McMary Marimba.

"Look guys I can vouch for where The Viscount has been the entire past evening, through the very early morning and right up to this minute," said the former Philly detective.

One of the herd of police officers said there had been an apparent murder on Simonton near Eaton and witnesses described a suspect as wearing weird clothing similar to what The Viscount wears.

"I've been with him and McMary here for the whole time. No way he would have gotten up into that palm tree," Obretta continued. "In fact, I slept here right in front of the door, because I too have been suspicious of him, even to the extent that I wanted to case his house after he and McMary went to bed."

"Did you find anything?" asked police Detective Robert ("Honey") Trapezzio, who was now heading the investigation of the head-coconut killing with the somewhat able assistance of Officer Chaz Lakestein.

"Yes, I did," said Obretta.

"What was that?" queried Officer Lakestein.

"The body of Shallaha Obbst."

"You gotta be shittin' me!" shouted Detective Trapezzio.

"Why didn't you inform us of this earlier?" asked Lakestein.

"Well, I wanted to question them when they got up," responded Obretta.

"What kind of asshole are you?" asked Trapezzio "You are no longer a detective. We can charge you with obstruction of justice. We let you off on that voyeurism charge in the cemetery because you were one of us. This time we won't be so nice."

"Look, I'm now convinced The Viscount and McMary had no knowledge of the body being in the next bedroom to theirs. It probably hadn't been there very long. Actually, the girl was still pretty warm when I discovered her. I even thought that when I pulled the palm tree frond from her mouth, I might be able to revive her. But no such luck," said Ted Obretta.

"I am convinced, as their witness, that the couple had absolutely nothing to do with Shallaha's death and certainly not the murder that you say just occurred on Simonton. Whose was that?" Obretta asked.

"It was a guy named Whitlow Wyatt, a guy from Buffalo, New York. He was jogging and was struck by a head and a coconut. They were flung at him from a tree. He didn't have a wallet but we were able to identify him from his Buffalo Bills medallion that had a picture of him and the former Bills coach, Marv Levy, on it. He must have been an ardent fan," said Lakestein, scratching his crotch.

"Hey that's one of my friends. We went on the trip to Key West together with two other guys. Jesus H. Christ, you go down here to relax and all this crap has to happen," said Ted, with eyes welling with water and looking to The Viscount and McMary for comfort.

Ted thought back to all the journeys he and his three friends had taken. If he had known foul play was to have happened to any of them, he would have taken more time to be with the guys the past week. They had always wanted to go to Key West together, Whit Wyatt, Charlie York and Zemblon Yurcocitch. And now this had to happen. He had better call Charlie and Zemblon and tell them the bad news. The other two had left the island, as planned, while Ted and Whitlow were to stay a few days longer, for two distinctly separate reasons, Ted investigating the growing crop of murder cases and Whitlow in love with Pansy Riviera. 'Oh my God,' Ted thought, 'I'll have to notify her as well. This is not going to be easy.'

Ted Obretta decided to walk over to The Gardens, the beautiful botanical inn of 17 rooms at the corner of Angela and Simonton. Most people don't know what the place looks like inside because of its white walled exterior. Once inside, though, one finds an arboretum of delicacies – a peace and loveliness that is modern but fits well into the Key West pattern of architecture and lifestyle. And the vegetation, the birds, the cats, the winding pathways and the two levels of balconied floors of inn rooms, all with varnished doors against white-planked walls and the green roofs, are easy on the eyes.

Ted asked at the front desk if he could have Whit Wyatt's room rung. No answer. Jody, the manager, had Barbara, one of her stellar assistants, check the room.

No one there. And nothing in the room, but a man's satchel and his shaving kit. No indication that Whit's girlfriend Pansy Riviera was coming back.

Ted went over to sit down on one of the chaise lounges by the big curving pool and tried to figure out what was going on. Why would she have gone? Whitlow Wyatt had gone out for an early morning jog, before 7 a.m. Why would his girlfriend just take off before he got back, that early in the morning? It was now not even 9:30 a.m. This did not make sense, Ted reasoned.

Was there harm done to her? Where did she go? He knew that the loving couple had planned to stay some extra days, just as he did.

When he checked back at the front desk, the word was that no one had seen the young woman leave the inn. Whitlow Wyatt had not indicated a check-out either for that day, not for a few days more.

Ted decided to call his friend Lovie, the Sheriff's deputy, to have his office check all the airlines to see if Pansy Riviera had made arrangements to leave the island. Not so.

She could have obviously left by some other means, but Ted just had one of those police hunches that she was still around. But where? And why? There wouldn't have been any palatable way for Pansy to have found out about her boyfriend's killing this fast. The police didn't know that Whitlow and she had suddenly decided to move to the Gardens. So she would not have as yet been contacted. Ted was the only person who knew where they were, as he had spent time with them at the bar at One Duval a couple nights earlier, and they had told him where they would be staying. They called it "hibernating."

The question in ex-Philly detective Ted Obretta's mind at this point: 'Was she in any way harmed or in danger or did she have something to do with her boyfriend's death or any of the other murders?'

Ted's mind ran amuck as he sat there on the chaise lounge amid the sanctuary of one of Key West's best inns, probably one of the best inns in the world.

❈

CHAPTER TWENTY-EIGHT

Heidi Hamms It Up In The Bay

BY NOW HEIDI HAMM was having a Rolling Rock on Johnny Gordon's ketch, still parked just off Christmas Tree Island. With her was Hreben Cruiz, one of the bikers she met on her way back from Boca Raton.

"Johnny always wanted to go to Costa Rico in this stupid tub," said Heidi. "He was getting sick of Key West and was thinking of moving to Costa to save money and maybe buy a house on an inlet where he could park his boat. The dumb ass could have done that – but not with me – and had his good time but the shit has to go and kill one guy and then himself over pure and simple jealousy. What a dick!"

"Well, I spose we can take his boat wherever we want to now, Heidi," said Hreben, who looked more like an Hispanic basketball player than a biker, with his long and angular 6-5 frame. The other guy, Weasel, looked the biker part, with thick, tattooed shoulders and a solid, girthy body.

They had been partying with Weasel Windsiege, the other biker since the previous night, with very little sleep.

Strange, Weasel wasn't still with them on the late Johnny's wooden 30-footer, which Johnny adored but never bothered to name. Johnny wouldn't have liked this scene at all, for he loved the ketch more than he did Heidi. At least he could trust the sailing craft with the double sails.

The two people who liked that boat the most were incapacitated – the now suicidally dead Johnny Gordon and his friend Zero Belinsky, now residing in the Monroe County Detention Center, under suspicion of murder.

Meanwhile, Heidi Hamm, Johnny's longtime off-again- on-again girlfriend and now widow, parties on.

Heidi was hanging with some tough critters in Weasel and Hreben. They're the guys who beat Robert Cleverly to a pulp outside the Bottle Cap and got away with it.

They've both had a string of short jail sentences for other beatings, drug possession, illegal possession of firearms and a variety of felonies and misdemeanors in the keys. They were bad asses of the first order, but no crime they committed put them into a league of truly dangerous criminals.

Yet, if one thought about it, he might consider them as suspects in some or perhaps all of the killings. They knew Costas Delupas. Used to buy and sell drugs in a long engagement of commerce with him at his A Taste of Bulgaria bake shop. They knew Shamir O'Neill, the fisherman/drug peddler, who found Delupas's body near the mangroves. Several of the other murdered folks were known to buy drugs from both Delupas and O'Neill.

Perhaps they murdered Delupas over some dispute and then realized that the other people who were subsequently murdered could have pointed fingers at them. Maybe, too, that was the reason for beating Cleverly to a pulp, for he, though he was new in town, had been at the bake shop the day before Delupas's body was found.

Well, at least one of them still could be a suspect. Weasel Windsiege was the next victim to bite the dust, or suck the water. Heidi and Hreben found Weasel hanging from the bowsprit of the boat. He was hanging upside down, ankles tied to the sprit, his head dangling in the Gulf water. He had a contusion on the back of his head but he died from drowning as the tide came in toward Christmas Tree Island that early morning. This must have happened in the wee hours of the morning when Heidi and Hreben were asleep for a short time.

❈

Ted Obretta had just heard about this murder while visiting Lovie Jones at the Sheriff's Office. He had gone over there to get whatever info he might find about the disappearance of Pansy Riviera. Jones had been called by the Coast Guard who were called by Heidi Hamm about the death of Weasel Windsiege.

"What's goin' on here?" asked Ted. "These all must be linked."

"I wouldn't jump to those conclusions if I were you, Obretta," said Deputy Jones. "I'll tell you one thing, though, we have more law enforcement people investigating everything than I've ever seen before. The police are trying to figure out who killed Whitlow Wyatt and some of the others and now I've got to add Weasel Windsiege, a real shitteroo who's caused me no end of trouble up and down the keys, to my caseload. The feds will be all over this one, too. They'll figure drugs were involved."

"You know, I've been following Heidi Hamm for the past three days and she may be the femme fatale in all this," said Obretta. "She's a looker with a hell of a body, wear's all that revealing stuff, and is just this side of a slut but she's smart as hell, too."

"You probably think she's implicated in a lot of this crap don't you?" questioned Deputy Jones. "You haven't been right on much, bro, but I think you may have something here. Think about it, where the hell was she when we had an all-points bulletin on her and Johnny Gordon when they disappeared for a week?"

"Well, maybe I should have a talk with her," said Obretta.

"Yeah, big-time detective... If you can catch her to talk," responded Jones.

"It would be my pleasure to try," Obretta said with a Sicilian smile.

Sure enough, by the time Ted Obretta got to the late Johnny Gordon's boat, there was no sign of Heidi or Hebren. After the Coast Guard arrived, removed the body of Weasel Windsiege, questioned the two of them and turned the investigation over to the Monroe County Sheriff's Office, they had been hauled in, interrogated for several hours and then mysteriously let go on their own recognizance. The theory was they might be suspects but there was not enough evidence that they were involved in the foul play. Deputy Lovie Jones was the one who let them go.

When Obretta found out they were let go he fumed.

"How can you just let them go?" he spouted to Jones.

"Look, retired shit, we didn't have anything realistic on them, and besides I thought, if they are involved, they might lead us to other people who are also involved in these crimes – the real culprits. And, Heidi Hamm may have some bad ass friends but she has no record, no trouble with the law at all. And a lot of people like her around town because she is a Key West character.

"I don't want to find myself quoted, or pictured, in *The Citizen*, and have this turn out to be a half-baked arrest that doesn't hold up," Deputy Jones continued.

"Well, what about Hebren Cruiz?" asked Obretta. "Wouldn't he be a good suspect?"

"Yeah, sure, killing his best friend of 20 years for no apparent reason. We know how to watch that guy up and down the keys. If he had something to do with the murder of Windsiege, we'd probably be able to find him fast, but I don't think he had anything to do with it. He weeped the entire time we interviewed him and Heidi. He even looked like he was going to slam Heidi a right hook when she started laughing during the interogation. She thinks everything is funny and she was infuriating him. I had to pull him apart from her."

Later that afternoon, Ted had a chance meeting with Robert Cleverly at the bar in P.T.'s, a favorite local hangout for food and suds on Caroline Street.

"How you been feelin' since you got out of the hospital?" Ted asked.

"Getting better," said Cleverly, who was now out of most of his bandages but still with his left eye appearing to be hanging out and his other eye slanting in a way that gave it an Asian look.

"You know we have a pretty good idea as to who beat you up," Obretta commented. "But I think it will be hard to prosecute them because no witnesses bellied up."

"Well, things are better for me since I found a girl who I've been dating," said Cleverly, with his usual air of smugness.

"In your condition that is quite a coup. She a local?" asked Ted.

"Yeah, her name is Heidi, Heidi Hamm. She said she'd meet here around three o'clock."

"You kiddin' me?... She's meeting you here?"

"What of it? I'm trying to act more like a local and this is the local spot. I asked Heidi to meet me at P.T.'s.

"Do you know much about her?"

"Not much, except she's great in the sack."

"How long have you known her?" asked Ted.

"Just met her two days ago but I feel like I've known her for years. Met her at the Garden of Eden, where she was getting her body painted. She told me to see her later that evening at the Green Parrot. I couldn't find her there, but I ran into her at La Concha Bar. Then we went over to my place and had a good time."

"For godsakes what makes you think she'll show up right now?" asked Ted, growing ever more frustrated. "She is totally unpredictable."

"I've got her cell phone," said Cleverly. "She goes nowhere without that."

"What did you do, steal it from her?" asked Ted furtively.

"Let's just say I appropriated it," replied Cleverly smugly.

"Well, I'd like to talk to her. She could be implicated in some of the murders that have occurred here the past week."

"You must be kidding, she never told me anything about them."

"Well, let me tell you something smartass, you could be the next one if you don't watch out. Six of them in the last week, whereas, Key West averages one every 10.4 years."

"Why do you think such a little cuddlebug like Heidi could be implicated in such heinous crimes?" asked Robert Cleverly.

"I don't know that she actually perpetrated any of them, but she might well have been close to the people that had, kapiche?"

With that, rather subtly, Cleverly placed his left hand on Obretta's right thigh.

Now there are some things you can get away with with a strapping, strong, late-fifties ex-detective from Philadelphia, but that's not one of them.

"What the fuck!" exclaimed Ted.

"You bring out the other side in me. When I was growing up in Grevey, Idaho, there weren't always that many girls around. We just sort of improvised as we later did up in Chicago in the ad biz," replied Cleverly.

"Listen you popeyed freak, you'll be back in the hospital or worse if you try to grope me again, you shit," Ted responded, with his dark eyes piercing through Cleverly.

"Look, just forget it, let's just be friends," said Cleverly, still with a sly grin, thinking Ted could still be had.

"Buddy, I'm not screwing around here, I want to find Heidi Hamm and damned fast."

"You will... in fact, here she comes," giving both Ted Obretta and Heidi Hamm sidelong glances in either direction.

"Hi, fagboy, howya doing!" said Heidi upon seeing her new boyfriend.

"Hello lovebug, you're about 45 minutes late."

"Go to hell, I was trying to get some of the body paint off from the other night when I saw you. Last night we had a little party on Johny Gordon's boat and one of the party animals turned up dead. You should have been there. And, who's the tough guy next to you?"

"Ted Obretta, he's a guy – a detective of sorts – who wants to talk with you, beauty," said Cleverly.

"Listen dweebs, I'm leavin' if I have to be with a detective. I just spent three hours talkin' to the sheriff's deputies. I've done nothing wrong."

"Yes, perhaps, but you seem to hang with some bad guns," opined Ted. "Do you know, doll, that there have been six murders in Key West in the past week, while Key West averages only one every 10.4 years, and in fact, there was once a 22.7-year period where no murder occurred at all?"

"Boy, that eighth month must have been brutal," snapped Heidi.

"It was, that's when a guy who balanced a refrigerator on his nose at the sundown ceremony at Mallory Square got so pissed off at a woman who was egging him on and then didn't give him a tip, he flung her against an ice cream cart and killed her. The guy was from Romania."

"How do you know so many odd facts and figures?" asked Cleverly, with a sly smile, showing several broken and missing teeth from the beating by the bikers.

"I've been hanging out with one of the longest-time Sheriff's deputies in the county," said Obretta. "He knows more crap about this town and the keys than anyone you can imagine."

At this point, Cleverly now had his left hand on Obretta's right thigh and his right on Heidi's left.

"Perhaps, we should have a menage a trois," said Cleverly with a smarmy grin, one eye looking at Ted, the other at Heidi, who herself looked lascivious, with her strawberry hair pulled back, her short cutoffs and a white tubetop against her deeply tanned skin.

With that, Ted got up and hammered Cleverly with a right to the pusser, knocking out another tooth or two as Cleverly fell to the bar floor. And it seemed only seconds that the Key West cops were in the place. They protected P.T.'s as well as any place because it was one of their favorite late night hangouts when off duty.

With all the commotion and Ted being handcuffed, Heidi slipped out of the place.

The cops at first didn't know who Ted was, just thought it was an afternoon bar fight they had to break up.

By the time everything settled down Heidi was long gone. She had no reason to be of any help to Ted, although as she scurried she thought she wouldn't mind doing him.

❈

CHAPTER TWENTY-NINE

Zero Is Out Of Jail; But There Are Revolting Developments At Sea

ALMOST AT THE SAME TIME Ted Obretta was being apprehended by the Key West cops, Zero Belinsky was being released by the Monroe County Detention Center for lack of evidence.

The Key West police were not happy about Ted messing up again. He was caught earlier for voyeurism and there was later the thought of charging him with obstruction of justice. Now a bar fight or shall we say coldcocking a patron.

"Look, guys, this sonofabitch was trying to put the make on me while I was seeking to obtain information from that woman, information that would help in the investigation of all these crimes the past week," said Ted, as Robert Cleverly writhed in pain on the floor.

One of the cops, Officer Jerome Weedrick, said, "You are not a cop; the whole department is talking about you. You seem to cause trouble everywhere you go, or get your nose into something you shouldn't."

Officer Weedrick, whose name is emblazoned on his squad car (a Key West police perk after you've been on the force for a couple of years), and a fellow officer, Harvey Ivy, were preparing to take Ted to jail, when the bartender interjected.

"This man didn't do anything wrong; it was the other guy, the one on the floor without the teeth and the bulging eyes," said the girl named Chrissie. "The guy on the floor had been making advances on the man you are trying to arrest and the man was clearly resisting them. That pervert down there even was suggesting a menage a trois with a girl who was with them. He had his hands on both their thighs; I could see everything."

"She's right, she's right!" shouted Obretta.

"Now, just calm yourself down," said Officer Weedrick, inadvertently stepping on Robert Cleverly's hand.

"Officer, this was a justified coldcocker if I've ever seen one. I'd have punched the guy too if he came on to me and I wasn't interested," said Chrissie.

"Well, then, I guess we'll let you off the hook again Obretta, but I'm telling you the whole damned force is watching you," Weedrick offered, and as he took the cuffs off of Obretta, he dropped them and they landed on Cleverly's nose, which was also bleeding from Ted's wallop. Ted has a large hand.

Then the cops picked up Cleverly and sat him down on a barstool. "Welcome to Key West," said Officer Ivy. "First you get beat up by bikers and then you try to make a big ex Philadelphia detective. You're lucky he only punched you once. He's got mitts the size of Muhammad Ali. Don't push him again. I don't think you're having very good luck in this town, would ya say?"

"Once you get your balance, we want you to go on home," said Officer Weedrick.

Robert Cleverly went on home.

Zero Belinsky, the one-armed midget plumber, who was under suspicion of the Costas Delupas murder was released from the detention center this day.

The Monroe County Sheriff's office decided it didn't have enough evidence in the case, and the prosecutor agreed.

Originally, they thought Zero might have been involved in the Delupas killing but also they implicated him in the disappearance of Johnny Gordon and Heidi Hamm. Now, Heidi had returned to Key West and Johnny Gordon was dead, at his own hand, slicing his own throat in a fashionable Boca Raton bar after stabbing to death another man in a jealous fit over Heidi.

Zero was glad to be out of jail but he pined over his good friend Johnny. He immediately sought the counsel of his rabbi, Otto Blintz, and his other friends Morky Golub and Seamus Fine. They had picked him up at the jail and then the four of them went to Mangoes on mid-Duval at Angela.

"I've been in jail all week, haven't seen *The Citizen*, haven't heard the radio, what's been happenin'? I knew about Johnny, 'cause they kept asking me questions about him and Heidi, then they told me Heidi showed up and Johnny was dead. How could this happen? I know I got caught schtumping Heidi on Johnny's boat, but I really liked the guy. We worked together every day and basically got along," said Zero.

"I'll tell you vhat's happenin'," said Rabbi Blintz. "Dey are droppin' like flies around here, like flies in a bad restaurant vhere da food is so bad it poisons the flies."

"What you mean, rabbi?"

"Vhat I mean is dat we have had six moiders here, all in one veek's time!" exclaimed Blintz.

"Some are gay, some are hetero, some I do not know vhat, but dey be droppin', honey," the rabbi added.

"Yeah, Zero, they have the drug agents, the alcohol, tobacco and firearms experts, the FBI, the state law enforcement people, the Navy military police, the Coast Guard and, last but certainly not least, the poison control people, the Key West police and the Monroe County Sheriff's deputies all in on the action. The only thing they don't have running around is the dogcatcher and the Moped Hospital," said Morky Golub.

"At least they can't hang the other five murders on you, Zero, since you were in the clink for everything except the Costas Delupas murder," said Seamus Fine.

"Anyhow, dey found out dat Costas vas keeled by poisoning and then someone must have throwed him off in the Gulf and den he got all mangled by a propeller blade and later Shamir O'Neill says he found his head out by the mangroves," said the rabbi. "A lot of crazy shit if you ask me."

Shamir had felt repentant about being the first to discover the headless body but not tell the authorities about it. Several days later he motored his yawl back into the mangroves, looking for the head. To his amazement he found it and he thought he now could do a good deed. He found the head wedged into the base of one of the thickly rooted trees. Then he took the head to the Coast Guard, feeling somewhat chastened, and once again was able to fish without too much guilt.

"Some louse even later stole da head and used it as a murder veapon to keel some touron," added the rabbi. "Who vould do dat? Who da hell vould throw a head from a tree to keel a touron vit it and also vit a coconut. Costas vould be real pissed if he knew vat dey're doin' vith his cabbage. The sonovvabeech probably used Costas's mustache as a twirling device to get more leverage to keel the stupid jogger.

"Dis is getting so crazy around here dat I might go back to Villiamsburg and sell fine hats dere in da Hasidic district. Dose hats come in real nice boxes, I remember. But I just hope dey catch the shit who's doin' dis. I vant paradise to return to my second home. But you jus relax, honey, you are off the hook now."

At Mangoes, the four friends continued to talk over straight up Beefeater martinis with anchovy olives.

"Dey makes da best big martinis in Key Vest," said the rabbi, toasting his friends at the shiny varnished outside bar, overlooking Duval.

The police investigating the Shallahah Obsst murder case pretty much believe in Ted Obretta's alibi that The Viscount and McMary couldn't have had a hand in the killing because they were with him the entire previous evening and into the next morning. And, by the way, he convinced them that the body was still somewhat warm shortly after The Viscount and McMary went to bed, meaning that the murder probably took place just before the three of them got back to the home on Duval at United.

He also convinced them that The Viscount had nothing to do with the head/coconut bludgeoning of Whitlow Wyatt later that morning, for he had been with The Viscount and McMary the entire night and he knew The Viscount did not leave the house. Yes, it was an imposter up in that tree who threw the head and coconut at Wyatt and summarily killed him. It was an imposter who was wearing the garb The Viscount was accustomed to wearing: usually a big hat of some type, a blue blazer with epaulets, gray cuffed shorts, black riding boots or cowboy boots and a hairy chest beneath the jacket (he almost never wore a shirt).

The Viscount said to McMary, "Why don't we take a ride down to Sloppy Joe's before the cruise ships come in and it's too crowded. I could quaff a few beers and maybe a shot of tequila or three with some nice salt and lime."

"Let's go!" returned McMary.

The Viscount waved to many of the people on the street as he and McMary rode west on Duval, heading for Sloppy Joe's.

It was about 9 a.m., and Big Mama, or Bonnie, her real name, greeted them as they entered Sloppy's. Big Mama is a tall, husky woman with short-cropped blonde hair and an always-pleasant personality. They were among the first to hit Sloppy's that morning. Everything glistens at Sloppy Joe's, the night crew cleaning it spotlessly from the hours of festivities the day and evening before.

"What's knew guys? Haven't seen you in a few days," said Big Mama or Bonnie, whichever you prefer.

Two other patrons on the other side of the "U"-shaped bar looked on with amusement as they tried to get themselves on the bar's web-site so the poor people back home could see them. One of the guys was tanned dark, swarthy, swilling a mug of beer. The other one, with a white beard, was having a beer as well. They appeared to be in their fifties and about as mature as two eleventh graders, laughing at the TV camera and peering at McMary and the strange guy she was with.

Not long after, Ted Obretta stopped in. He walked over to McMary Marimba and The Viscount and gave them each a strong hug. These three had bonded warmly after the ordeals they had been through the past week.

"It is good of you to spend so much time helping out with the murders," said McMary, her dark brown hair flowing and glistening.

"Well at first I think the police and sheriff's deputies thought I was just a nosey ex-cop trying to get my jollies but now with the weight of all these cases in a week, I don't think they mind having an extra detective around," replied Ted, reaching for his Key West lager. "Plus, I come cheap… I'm even paying for my expenses."

"Do you have any idea of who the killer or killers

might be?" asked McMary.

"It's all puzzling. We think we have some people who might know what happened and why, but they might not necessarily have perpetrated the crimes," said Ted.

As Ted talked, The Viscount couldn't lay his eyes off of his squeeze. He was more than oblivious to the train of the conversation. It was a hot day, even hitting a good 90 degrees this early morning.

"Hey T.V. are you missing any clothes? I'll bet you a dollar that the person who killed Shallaha Obbst in your spare bedroom also made off with one of your outfits," Ted told The Viscount. "But I'll bet whoever it was doesn't look as handsome as you – and isn't as courteous as you either."

"Thank you for the compliment, T.O.," said The Viscount. "McMary did find one of my winter outfits missing. That guy in the tree must have been sweating up a storm. He took one of the outfits I wear when we go to the south of Chile in our sailing egg competition. Those clothes are made for the winters of Antarctica. Very heavy indeed. I'm surprised the guy could even get up into that palm tree."

"Well, whoever it was was a strong sucker," Ted said, waving Big Mama over for another ice cold lager.

When Big Mama came over she asked the three if they might like to go fishing. "It's early enough. My husband is a great sport fisherman. Just had a cancellation at the last minute. Wanna go?"

"You know what Bonnie?... that's a good idea," said Ted. "All I've been doing on my vacation is work for free. It's time to have some fun. What do you say McMary and T.V.?... you wanna go out for the day?"

"Count us in," said McMary. "The Viscount's never been fishing since he's been here."

"Might like to go spear fishing; that's what we do off the Isle of Goda. That would be hard here though because I don't have a spear," remarked The Viscount with a chuckle.

"Don't worry, my husband has all the tools on deck," Bonnie/Big Mama replied.

"Let's go," said Ted. And they left, leaving the two guys in their fifties the only people at the sprawling Sloppy Joe's bar that morning. One of the guys was talking on his cell phone and waving to the camera to somebody back home who was watching them on the Internet.

Soon Sloppy's would be inundated with throngs from the two big cruise ships that had arrived that morning just south of Mallory Square on the Gulf of Mexico, and a guy named Barry Cuda would be entertaining them on the honky tonk piano. Such is the endless life at Sloppy Joe's.

❊

Not long after The Viscount, Ted and McMary cruised westward from the Key West Marina, near Garrison Bight, something stunning happened.

They had not even gotten to the little inlet that would allow them the expanse of the Gulf of Mexico when a whooshing sound indicated something was amiss.

The Viscount wouldn't have to look for an extra spear, for now one was sticking through his big black hat with the silver buckle around it, narrowly missing its target.

But the target was probably not The Viscount but instead Ted Obretta who was standing right next to The Viscount below the captain's deck. The spear knocked off The Viscount's hat and stuck it up against the wall of the cabin.

No way to tell exactly where the spear had come from as there were many boats at dock this morning and quite a few others going out to sea. For all one knew it could have come from the water in the bight, which is located just to the northwest of the Old Town district of Key West. Someone could have shot the spear gun and then ducked under water and swum to a hiding place amongst the many boats.

"That was meant for me!" Ted shouted. "If I hadn't bent down to the left to help put the fishing poles in place it would have hit me in the square of the back. You were lucky it got only your hat."

The Viscount had been standing a step below looking out to sea when the spear swooshed in and stuck the hat right above the door going to belowdecks.

"Duck down, duck down!" yelled McMary. "They may have more spears!"

"I don't think so," said Ted calmly as The Viscount pulled his hat and the spear out of the varnished wooden plank above the belowdecks door.

"I can tell you this: It's one operative, not more. We'd have gotten a spray of spears if there were more than one person out there," rationed Ted.

"Somebody wants me. Someone who figures I know too much or will know too much as I go about this investigation. I can't even go fishing without getting involved with this mess," Ted continued.

The Viscount was now holding his own spear gun in a protective guerilla stance at the stern of the big fishing boat, a remarkable 1950s Chris Craft mahogany cruiser that looks so much more majestic than the fiberglass/plastic tubs of today.

"I hate to give up this fishing trip but we had better head back in and report this incident," said Ted Obretta. "Lovie Jones, the sheriff's deputy on these cases will love to hear this one. At least he didn't have the seventh murder of the week on his hands."

And as he said that, another spear from a more diagonal direction came flashing in and nailed The Viscount's hat again, this time taking it into the water.

"That one was for me I think," said The Viscount.

"It was," said Ted. "You really shouldn't be standing there in a guerilla position. Whoever this is thinks you are trying to protect me. They'll take you out to get to me. Go belowdecks at once, go with him McMary, who said to Ted, "You know The Viscount's a brave man."

"He's going to be a brave dead man if he doesn't watch out!" Ted yelled. "Both of you get belowdecks now, and give me that gun, T.V."

Ted nestled into the stairwell and kept sight for any strange maneuverings around the marina and the bight.

"Hey, can I get my hat?" yelled The Viscount, whose big black chapeau with the silver buckle was floating out toward sea.

"Look, just stay down there you sonofabitch. I'm going to have enough trouble protecting myself if more spears are coming our way."

"But it was given to me by my great grandfather who was one of the early settlers of Parma Heights, Ohio. He came in on a horse with that big black hat.

It's been handed down!" yelled The Viscount. As a boy I came all the way from the Isle of Goda with my parents to have the passing down ceremony at my great grandfather's nursing home up there in Cheviot, Ohio."

"If your great grandfather settled Parma Heights, why was he in a nursing home in Cheviot?"

"He got a better deal there," answered The Viscount.

"Look, you already have two big holes in that big and treasured hat. The next hole will probably be in you!"

With that The Viscount brushed past Ted and dove off the cruiser and started swimming toward the hat, which now somehow had gotten past the little inlet that goes out to the Gulf. He kept swimming like an Olympian as McMary sat belowdecks in tears.

"That sonofabitch," muttered Ted, as another spear hit the boat. This one came from yet another direction.

And out at sea, from the west, dark clouds were forming.

"Jesus H. Christ," said Ted. "McMary, I've got spears coming at me from every direction and your little turd of a lover has to pull this stunt.

"I can only save the two of us and the captain. In police work you can only do so much. You always go for the larger mass instead of just one individual. I'll have the captain call the Coast Guard. They're the only people who will go out if that storm coming at us is as bad as the captain and I think. For now, we're heading back to dock, and I'm calling the Key West police."

And another spear came into the boat. This one piercing through the back of the seat in front of the lower deck steering wheel. Ted was mystified as to whether the spears were coming from the water or from other boats, or both.

He knew it was time to get back to the moorings, and there was not much he could do for The Viscount, who was still swimming after his heirloom hat and into the storm.

❁

CHAPTER THIRTY

Heidi And Pansy, Damsels In Deep Danger

When Ted Obretta and the others got back to the dock, with no more spears coming their way, he called Lovie Jones at the Monroe County Sheriff's Office. Another deputy told him that Lovie wasn't there at the moment. He was on assignment but was expected back soon. Ted said he would call back in a half-hour and told the deputy that he had notified the Key West police about the spearshooter or spearshooters. Ted wasn't sure just what had happened out in Garrison Bight.

But Ted couldn't wait. He decided to call Jones's cell phone. Jones was pissed and couldn't understand why Ted had to call in the middle of a detail. As usual Jones got through his initial fit at Ted's intrusions and told him he had been trying to track down Heidi Hamm and Pansy Riviera all day. "Heidi can provide more info if I can find her, and I have to tell you that I'm worried about Pansy, her welfare."

"Well, maybe you are going to have to worry about mine," Ted shouted back. "Somebody or some people have tried to take me out with a spear gun over the last couple of hours. They may even have tried to knock off The Viscount and even McMary Marimba, but I think the real target was me."

"Listen you abject fool," said Jones. "You shouldn't have gotten involved in any of this. You should have just taken your vacation like a good boy and you wouldn't be a target of any kind."

"You listen, Jones; one of my best friends, Whit Wyatt, was taken out by the perpetrator or perpetrators. There are a good six murders in a week here and there could be more than that. We could find more bodies or someone else could be targeted even as we speak, just like I was this morning," Ted growled.

"I'll tell you one thing," he continued, "Heidi Hamm could be the slipperiest little devil I've come across in a long time. I almost had her cornered and she disappears on me at P.T.'s. In a way, I think she is just playing with us. She might not have anything to do with the killings. She may have no knowledge of who is involved with them."

"Well, I want to track her down and try to interrogate her further. I let her go when that biker was murdered, Weasel Windsiege. I had to let her go because we had no evidence or the least bit of a motive," said Jones.

"Look, you're so involved with everything now, why don't you just hook up with me and we'll both see if we can find Heidi. And I sure as hell want to know what happened to the girlfriend of Whitlow Wyatt. Why she just disappeared right after his death. Doesn't make sense," Jones continued.

"Tell me where to meet you and I'll be there," said Ted.

"Meet down at Magnolia's. I need to get something to eat."

❖

It was about 2 p.m. in the afternoon when the two cops met at the cool little restaurant on mid-Duval.

They both figured that Heidi Hamm and Pansy Riviera were still on the island. Let us call it a cop's hunch.

After lunch, the two rode around for a couple of hours trying to think of where they might be able to find Heidi, who especially might have information or had overhead information that might be helpful to the cases. Their hands were tied in some respects because most of the murders were the investigations of the Key West police. However, seeing that the perpetrators could be anywhere up and down the keys, the Monroe County Sheriff's Office had good reason to keep pursuing its own investigation.

Then they thought the best bet for contacting Heidi was through her and the late Johnny Gordon's friend, Zero Belinsky. The likeable little one-armed plumber would be easy to find.

They decided to walk down Duval to Rabbi Otto Blintz's cottage on Dupont Lane. They figured that they might find Zero there, since he just got out of jail and might have been picked up by the rabbi. On the way down, they didn't have to go to the cottage. They spotted the rabbi with Zero, both of whom were still at Mangoes outdoor bar with Morky Golub and Seamus Fine.

"You are off the hook," said Deputy Jones. "I didn't think we had that much crap on you in Costas's murder and you couldn't have been involved with the rest 'cause you were in the old clinker when they happened.

"This is my buddy Ted Obretta. You may have met him briefly before. He's helping out on these cases out of good service to mankind, since he is a retired Philadelphia detective."

Ted nodded to the guys he had met earlier in the week. He had also talked briefly with Zero Belinsky after Zero was incarcerated.

"Zero, we are trying to find Heidi Hamm," Ted said. "You know her quite well I've heard. Where do you think she is?"

"I'd probably look for her at Johnny Gordon's boat,"

said the one-armed midget plumber who also was a Hemingway look-a-like. "She usually ends up there after partying somewhere else. I'm not sure she really has a home in Key West. If you want I'll take you to the boat."

"Yeah, go boy!" said Morky. "You be a detective now. You help these guys out and maybe you'll stay out of jail."

"Yeah," said Seamus. "We'll keep enjoying our drinks here and you help them find Heidi."

"Hey, let me go vith you," said Rabbi Blintz. "I know Heidi pretty vell too. She'll talk to me. Long time ago vhen Johnny Graham vas on a fishin' trip Heidi and I vent up and spent a couple nights in Largo. A good time vas had by all, if you know vhats I mean. Heh, heh."

"I think it is safe to go over to Christmas Tree Island. That storm we encountered in the late morning blew over fast. My guess is that The Viscount found his hat and the Coast Guard found him," said Obretta looking up to the western sky. "Can you believe that jackass jumps off a boat and goes after a goddamned hat in a raging storm while we are being pelted with spears?" he asked Deputy Lovie Jones as the group left Mangoes.

They got in a Sheriff's water cruiser and motored out through the choppy bay to the location of Johnny Gordon's boat, just off Christmas Tree Island.

As they got closer to Johnny's boat they saw the figures

of two women, one short and blonde and one taller with dark hair, standing near the helm. It looked like the two were preparing to cast away. And it was apparent that the two were Heidi Hamm and Pansy Riviera. Everybody knew Heidi, and Jones and Obretta were able to identify Pansy from earlier contact with her.

Why would Pansy be hanging out with Heidi shortly after her new boyfriend had been murdered? How did they even know each other? Simply put, what was going on?

Jones yelled at Heidi that they wanted to come on board to ask her some questions and also they had some questions for Pansy as well.

They rafted the Sheriff's boat onto Johnny's and came aboard, Deputy Lovie Jones, Ted Obretta, Zero Belinsky and Rabbi Blintz.

"Hey, Zero, it's good to see you and I'm glad you're out of jail," yelled Heidi to her three-foot-eight friend with the one arm.

"Hi, Heidi," returned the midget, "these guys want to talk with you. You can help in the investigations of the murders."

"Yeah," said Jones, "we don't think you are implicated but you know a lot of people, some people who might have a reason to have been involved with the murders."

"And, I'd like to know why you took off right after or before your boyfriend was murdered, Miss Riviera," added Jones.

"Pansy, I can't believe you would just disappear when our mutual friend was wasted," said Obretta.

Pansy looked down and didn't answer. She appeared that she might be under the influence of some substance, maybe Quaaludes and some high-powered tequila. Several bottles of Cuervo Gold and bowls of limes and salt were on the counter, Ted observed. Her legs were wobbly.

Ted was beginning to think that Pansy had something to do with the death of her boyfriend. His suspicion meter had pressed beyond the 100 percent mark, and he blurted out, "Look, chick, I want you to talk and talk fast. You could be implicated in the murder of Whitlow Wyatt and your ass is going to be on the line if you don't cooperate."

Pansy looked up briefly and murmured, "I don't know who killed Whitlow, I don't know. I just want to go back to Iowa," she said, her dark Eurasian features beautiful even in such despair.

"Hey, Pansy, you don't have to tell these guys anything," informed Heidi. "You have nothing to hide and you know nothing, only that your boyfriend was killed."

"Shut up," said Obretta. "We'll decide which way

this conversation is going to go."

Deputy Jones then read both of the women their rights and the questioning went on.

"Heidi, how much do you know about the motorcycle guys, the one who was killed, Weasel Windsiege, and Hreben Cruiz? What do you know about their connection with Robert Cleverly, the new guy in town?" asked Obretta.

"Just that they beat the shit out of him, but the police can't prove anything and I wasn't there so I am a shit-bird witness," replied Heidi, her muscular body twitching for more tequila.

"No, that's not what I mean. Were those three connected in any drug action in any way?" countered Obretta.

"I don't know a damned thing. You people always think I know something when I don't."

"Listen, Heidi, you must co-operates vith da fuzz; it eel be better for you and you can help vith da investigation," blurted Rabbi Blintz.

"Rabbi, I know how to cooperate, but when I do that, it is more in the horizontal position," chirped Heidi, as the four men ogled her ample cleavage.

Deputy Jones seemed to be content with Ted asking all the questions, apparently figuring Ted had more experience with big-time crime. And Ted was on a roll, just like in the old days as a detective in Philadelphia.

"Heidi, do you think the six killings were connected? Costas Delupas, The Pelican, Gary Bluett, Shallaha Obbst, Whitlow Wyatt and Weasel Windsiege?" Ted queried.

"Hell if I know. I have another date with Robert Cleverly this afternoon. Life goes on. I really can't help you," she said.

"Well, maybe I should go on that date with you," said Ted Obretta. "Maybe I could continue to ask you both some more questions."

"A menage a trois, I would like that," said Heidi. "You are Mr. Kinky, aren't you Ted, beneath that stern exterior. Let's make it 5 p.m."

"Knowing you, you wouldn't show up," riposted Ted. "You wouldn't show up... to torment Robert Cleverly and further screw up our investigation."

Pansy seemed to be suddenly growing more sober. She was weeping, with big tears swelling out of her black eyes.

"I, I, I have to tell you something" she said with mounting courage. "I know who the killer of all these people is. I know... I know... I know. He had an accomplice, too, as she pointed her right index finger out toward Rabbi Otto Blintz.

Commotion ensued, with the rabbi beginning to use vulgar language and denying all guilt. "I have nothings to do vith any of dee killings you gook," he said harshly. "You little sheet whooo-ore, you rancid placenta!"

As the rabbi ranted, Lovie Jones flipped out his .45 and pointed it at the group. He fired twice, hitting and exploding a bottle of tequila and sending the other bullet through the boat's windshield while Ted stood there stupefied.

In the burst of a few seconds, Zero came around from behind and kicked Deputy Jones hard right behind the left knee, buckling it and sending Jones to the floor of the ketch. Ted was about to pounce on Jones, who he thought was his friend and a good deputy, but was quickly repulsed by the rabbi's headbutt to his groin. This gave Jones the time to get up, throw himself into the Sheriff's boat and rip off the rafting to Johnny's ketch.

The Sheriff's stout, steel-hulled boat could do a good 60 knots. Jones spun away and made a giant U-turn, and then with the Sheriff's boat picking up speed aggressively he aimed it toward the wooden ketch, probably thinking he could knock off all of these witnesses and his one accomplice at once. The crash would hardly do any damage to the Sheriff's boat and he could speed away until he had time to make up a story to get himself off the hook.

The impact of the crash could be heard all the way

across the Gulf bay to Turtle Kraals and the Half Shell, a good mile and a half away.

Johnny's boat disintegrated like balsa wood and Deputy Jones just kept going northward, leaving the boat splinters in his wake.

❋

CHAPTER THIRTY-ONE

A Wild Race Ensues

Ted quickly had grabbed the two girls and dove with them toward Christmas Tree Island. Zero had no choice but to jump in the eight-foot high waters himself. He had cleared himself away from the crash but now found himself floundering in a circular motion, not being able to go in any particular direction what with having only one arm. The rabbi was less fortunate. He was not as spry as the others and just as he was readying to jump, the Sheriff's boat cut through the mid-section of Johnny's ketch, slingshotting the rabbi seventy feet into the air and landing him atop one of the fur trees on Christmas Tree Island.

"Eeeeeeeee Yoyeeeeeeeeee!" were the rabbi's last words.

Once Ted Obretta knew he had Heidi Hamm and Pansy Riviera in a safe spot on the island's shore, he went back to save Zero Belinsky. The little guy was still spinning in a circle but now more in sort of a whirlpool. As he was going down for the third and last time, Ted grabbed the midget's right and only arm and began yanking him to shore. Zero was saved but by now had swallowed a lot of saltwater. When he reached shore, Zero was both barfing and farting the seawater from his system.

Ted had saved himself and three other people from the ravages of a friend who tried to kill all of them.

The two young women thanked him profusely. Zero was still busy expunging the saltwater, and Ted was confused.

"I wish somebody could tell me what is going on. You take a 25-year deputy sheriff with a sterling record and he turns out to be the killer of six people. One of you girls must know something about this," he said, with a growing fatigue retching his body.

"I can tell you that Deputy Jones started to think we may have been too close to the investigation," said Pansy Riviera. "He had had us in as witnesses the better part of two days. Whitlow began thinking that all the murders were connected and I know he wanted to go to the Key West police and explain his suspicions. He somehow inferred that Deputy Jones was involved. He was sure it had to do with drugs. The day before he died he had called me at our room to explain that he was going to go to the police. Jones must have had the room phone tapped. He must have found out where we were staying.

"The morning Whitlow was killed, the rabbi came to our inn and said he had something he wanted to tell me about the investigation and he said he thought it would be best if Whit and I left town soon. He took me over to Johnny Gordon's boat for the time being where he said he thought I'd be safe. He said Heidi would take care of me until he could find Whitlow before any harm came to him. Whit was out on a jog when he was killed you'll remember. I told the rabbi he was out jogging, and the rabbi said he'd go out and try and find Whitlow before he ran into trouble. The Rabbi never came back until now.

"I'm sure Deputy Jones was going to come out and kill me too, and the rabbi helped him by setting me up. I think he was planning to kill Heidi, too, because he thought she knew too much as well. As far as I'm concerned Heidi had nothing to do with this. She was just dooped."

Just as Pansy Riviera finished her explanation, a voice came out of the woods.

"Jolly Ho, Jolly Ho." It was The Viscount, who had come out of the woods to find out what all the commotion was about.

"My God," said Ted, "I thought we had lost you to the storm after you started to swim after that silly hat. A lot has happened since then. My God, you show up at the strangest moments."

"The storm took me out to sea in a rapid current.

Every time I thought I had my hat, it would go beyond my reach. I finally caught up with it on Christmas Tree Island. Once I got here, and the storm had subsided, I was rather tired and fell asleep under one of the trees. It was a nice slumber because I knew I had in my possession the great hat of antiquities," said The Viscount.

"We've got a big problem," said Ted. "Lovie Jones is out to kill us. He took off in the Sheriff's boat after breaking Johnny Gordon's ketch in two but I wouldn't be surprised if he comes back. He knows we're on the island, and if he can keep us from leaving, he'll have his prey nicely in hand."

Indeed, that was what Lovie Jones was thinking. But he had a problem and that was that the impact knocked the steering mechanism of the Sheriff's boat awry and made maneuvering sluggish. So as he passed by one of the marinas he quickly docked the Sheriff's boat, grabbed a Sea-Do and raced back to the island. He brought a shotgun and a couple of spear guns with him.

But by then, Ted Obretta hailed a cruiser that was moored off Christmas Tree. He yelled to The Viscount to come with him to the dock to get a couple of Sea Dos. Ted thought this would be the best way to head off Jones.

He then instructed Zero to stay on the island with the two girls and protect them as best he could. That said, the little guy begot a perverse squint in his dark eyes, thinking the most salacious of thoughts. This could be fun, he thought, as long as the deputy doesn't come back after them.

Ted Obretta thought it was best for the other three to stay on the island, rather than risk having the whole group together, which would make it easier for Jones to knock 'em all off.

Ted and The Viscount got themselves two Sea-Dos at the boat basin next to the Ocean Reach Hotel at the lower end of Duval.

He told the rental boy, "We'll take 'em for two hours" and paid the kid in advance with his gold American Express card, which was past due and wouldn't process, but, now breathless, he convinced the kid they would not steal the boats and he'd make good on the rentals.

Ted decided to chase after Deputy Jones. Ted was so pissed off at Jones, his friend, supposedly, that he wanted to apprehend the mother himself, with perhaps a volunteer effort from The Viscount. At this point, his macho, ego and validation were at stake to him, and he was not about to let legitimate law enforcement authorities get in the way.

"Ted, let me help you chase him down," said The Viscount. "I'm good at sea and I can be a decoy to help route this evil man out."

"O.K., but just remember he is probably armed and

totally dangerous. You are doing this as a volunteer, not because I suggested anything," Ted instructed.

"Lovie won't have any help from the rabbi on this one. That guy is hanging quite appropriately from his britches on one of those Christmas trees," Ted continued. "I think the two of us can take Lovie out, but just watch your ass!"

With that Ted Obretta and The Viscount sped back toward Christmas Tree Island. The Viscount was scared but didn't want to show it. This time, he made sure to use the chin lariat of his great black hat with the silver belt, to keep it from falling into the sea. It had two big holes in it from the spears shot his way earlier, but it still was his treasure and, perhaps, good luck charm.

So they took off from the boat basin at One Duval just as one of the glass bottom boats was going out to sea with a couple hundred sight-seers. They got up to speed quickly and cut off the big glass bottom, giving the onlookers a sight of rip roarin' Key West.

Ted thought they should turn right and head toward the north. And they headed toward Christmas Tree Island, passing by Sunset Key, the key of beautiful expensive homes that is only accessible by boat. The Viscount commented to himself that perhaps he and McMary could some day live on Sunset, having tranquility and a wonderful modern home at the same time. The Viscount was apt to daydream even on board a Sea-Do going close to seventy miles an hour.

Ted Obretta kept signaling with his left arm for The Viscount to catch up with him as they headed toward Christmas Tree Island just to the north now. Ted wasn't sure he'd find Jones in the waters there, but it was a good place to start. He knew he and The Viscount didn't have much time.

He knew Jones might try to find the five of them again before he made flight from Key West, after the authorities were notified.

Jones, in fact, thought that they might all be hiding somewhere on Christmas Tree or maybe Ted was smart and asked a boater moored nearby to take him back to shore to tell the authorities. Ted might leave the others behind, Jones thought, because Ted would think it would be safer for the others to secret themselves on the island while Ted went for help.

Jones thought he would try to find Ted before he got back to land, take care of that little detail, then head back to Christmas Tree and snuff the others, thus eliminating all remaining witnesses.

The sea "motorcycle" he had appropriated was particularly quick and certainly would present a challenge to Obretta and The Viscount, who were riding rental grade Sea-Dos that probably didn't go as fast. But there were two of them against one, though the one had the artillery and a speedier, more maneuverable vehicle. This would probably be a contest nonetheless.

Suddenly, Ted felt a spear whiz by his left shoulder and then another over his right, this one sticking through The Viscount's hat, as The Viscount was right behind Ted west of Christmas Tree. Some good luck charm. The grand black hat with the silver buckle band now had three holes through it, but The Viscount persevered behind Ted all the while the spear was sticking through his beloved hat. He was afraid to pull it out and risk losing the hat again at this high speed.

Ted gathered all the acceleration his Sea-Do would allow heading right toward Deputy Lovie Jones. He stuck his right leg out to try to kick Jones off his jet ski. He missed and then, emulating Ted, The Viscount tried the same trick and toppled into the water at about 60 mph. He bounced and bounced for about 50 yards but came up bobbing in the water with his black hat still intact.

Jones made a sweeping U-turn and headed right toward The Viscount, figuring he could knock out one of these two guys and then go after the other. He conjured he had better do it quickly because soon the entire phalanx of law enforcement agencies would be after him. Yet he thought maybe the rest of the living witnesses were still on the island, and they could do nothing without phones, having left their cells on the shelf in Johnny's disintegrated boat.

He ran right over The Viscount who was still bobbing in the water. Ted figured that this was the end of another friend, as an expanding pool of blood whirled where The Viscount had been in the water. Ted thought that The Viscount might have been decapitated.

And now, Jones came right at Ted, readying another spear. This one missed by two feet but now Jones threw the spear gun into the salt waters and picked up the shotgun, which offered much greater degree of error. He shot one blast at Ted. And another.

Ted decided he had no alternative but to head right for Jones and try to knock him off the jet ski while Jones was reloading the shotgun. He had no choice because he would be a sure goner if he didn't make this last ditch effort. His Sea-Do and his wits were the only thing he had left.

He rumbled over the three-foot waves that were the remnants of the earlier storm and headed directly at the deputy who was still fiddling with the shotgun. Ted nicked Lovie sidelong and knocked him from the jet ski, flinging the shotgun into the water.

The two men went after each other, thrashing through the waves. Ted went for an eye-gouge and another, breaking a finger in the process. Then he tried a karate chop to the neck, breaking the rest of his hand. In return, the powerful Deputy Jones just banged Ted as hard as he could to the side of the head. Another punch to the other side of the head and then an uppercut took Ted into a world of stars, stripes, and multi-colored petunias, his mouth agape and taking in sea water.

Jones thought one more whack and he'd be rid of

his nemesis. And he plastered Ted once more and left him to be the food for the natural predators, the assertive species of sharks and barracudas in the Gulf. Surely, Lovie thought his work was done except for taking out the other three witnesses. As he mounted his jet ski to return for the others on Christmas Tree Island, or so he thought, he was stung by the twisting of a lariat around his neck. It twisted tighter and tighter until his eyes bulged. His only hope was to try to disable the assailant behind him. He did, three times, and the lariat loosened. The assailant was The Viscount, who was presumed dead, but instead knocked silly when the jet ski ran over him. The blood was from a 300-pound tarpon that took the brunt of the hit.

As Ted's body floated out into the Gulf, it was now left for The Viscount and Lovie Jones to duke it out.

"You mother, you holy mother!" yelled Lovie Jones.

"No, sir, my name is The Viscount," returned T.V., rubbing his damaged ribs.

"You're going down this time, you little freak!" excoriated Jones. With that, he landed a blow to The Viscount's solar plexus, and a hard wallop to the chin, knocking The Viscount off the back of Jones's jet ski and into the water, bubbles encircling The Viscount. Jones knew The Viscount would surely drown, or, like Ted, be taken by the predators of the sea.

Now it was time to take care of the others.

CHAPTER THIRTY-TWO

Carnage On Christmas
Tree Island?

LOVIE JONES, THE ERSTWHILE sheriff's deputy of 25 years, was hell bent on one thing: wiping out the remaining witnesses. He could explain these killings, if asked, and just tell his colleagues at the Sheriff's Office that the perpetrators were still at large. He could say that he had just missed catching them. He could make up many stories and they would be believed; after all, he was an oldtimer with almost no negative reports in his file. And he might even suggest that Ted Obretta, who was now "missing" had something to do with all this, and maybe The Viscount did as well.

This was the biggest crime spree in Key West history, not perhaps counting the pirates' escapades of a couple hundred years' yore.

Lovie Jones sped to Christmas Tree Island to find the others, not necessarily an easy task. Though the island is small, it is densely thick of the evergreen trees. There are largely no trails and these critters would be hard to find, he thought. He found his shotgun in the water and still had an extra spear gun on the jet ski. Lovie Jones was ready.

Since Johnny's boat was moored at the east end of the island before it was smashed in half by Deputy Jones, the deputy decided that the people who jumped off the boat, his prey, would probably go to the other end. He was right.

When he entered the island from the west, he heard much laughter and carrying on. He thought that these witnesses were having themselves a very good time. What fools, he thought, making it so easy for him to find them.

He went inward on the island toward where the noise was coming from. They'd never notice him approaching, he thought. This would be easy. Maybe three shotgun blasts and his work would be done.

And suddenly a swinging rope with a little man on it approached him from behind echoing:

"Taaaaaarrrrrrrrrrzzzzzzzannn, A-Hole... hole... hole... hole... yipeeeeee... yipeeee... Tarzan, Tarzan," yelped the voice behind Jones, and with that Jones was flattened to the island floor, small thorns sticking in his face. He was knocked out for a second or two, got himself up and groped for his guns.

But the midget, Zero Belinsky, punched him in the nuts with his strong right, and only, arm, and Jones buckled.

Writhing in pain and his breath taken from him, Jones nonetheless decided there was no way he would be taken out by a dwarf, and as he regained his strength, he reached for his shotgun, picked it up and slammed the butt of it between the little guys dark eyes. Zero fell to the ground as Lovie turned the gun around and aimed it downward, thinking that there would be pieces of the little prick all over the island in just a second or two.

Then as if a log had struck the backs of his knees, Lovie Jones toppled over in retching pain, the ligaments of both knees severed, but not before his shot gun went off and the pellets of which tore off Zero's one and only arm but not taking his life.

And then The Viscount began whacking Lovie Jones about head with his beloved black hat, the silver buckle of which scored welts on Lovie's forehead.

"You thought you had us both, didn't you and then you were going to kill the others, but we got you instead, you rotten ogre," yelled The Viscount in a voice more strident than anyone would have thought him capable of.

"You sonofabitch wannabe faggot," whimpered Jones. "I thought I had you. I shoulda shot you too instead of just drowned you, bro. You took out my knees to get back at me, you sonofabitch."

"I took out your knees in a special technique I learned in Isle of Goda feetball. You always do that to an opponent who does not play the game fairly. The technique involves rolling oneself into a veritable ball and racing behind the opponent with gusto and then at the last minute becoming straight as a cedar plank and taking him out," explained The Viscount.

"Well, at least," said Jones, in between low moans and murmers, "I got that half-assed retired detective Obretta. Sent him on a permanent vacation in the Gulf. I told him he should have stayed away from all this and now look where he is."

"He's right behind me, dork," said The Viscount, using the strongest word he has ever used.

Lovie Jones looked up and sure enough there was Ted Obretta standing behind The Viscount.

"I'm placing you under citizen's arrest, Jones," said Obretta. I'm not sure what the motives were for all this mayhem but I am certain that you and the rabbi were the only perpetrators. And I think it was all about cheesy, pente ante drug peddling. You are a disgrace to this badge," as he ripped Lovie Jones's medallion off his sheriff's shirt.

Ted did not look at all good. His face was as swollen as an over-inflated soccer ball.

"It was all about cheesy, pente ante drug peddling," he repeated as he looked down at former Deputy Jones.

❋

Postscript

Indeed it was all about drugs and avarice.

All of those murdered had been customers of Costas Delupas's drug business. All Deputy Lovie Jones wanted, after years of protecting Delupas the baker's side business was 13%, not a large sum for all the protection Jones provided and he had done it for nothing for the first 15 years.

Jones became so infuriated with Delupas the past year when he thought Delupas was cheating him out of some of his vigorish that he decided to rat poison the Bulgarian baker/drug peddler. Then he dropped Delupas's body into the mangroves, only to have it inadvertently chopped up by Shamir O'Neill, another drug peddler unconnected to the Delupas/Jones ring but nonetheless another schmuck.

The Pelican, Gary Bluett, Shallaha Obbst, Weasel Windsiege had all been customers of Delupas. They were long-time users and they knew who protected Costas Delupas and his customers. Whitlow Wyatt, Jones thought, had become too suspicious of Jones after two days of questioning by Jones. Jones also thought Pansy Riviera, Whitlow's'girlfriend, knew too much or thought she knew too much as well.

And, of course, everyone knew Heidi Hamm knew too much, so she had to go as well.

Some wonder why Jones would put on the garb of The Viscount and climb up a palm tree and then throw Costas Delpus's head along with a traditional coconut at Whit Wyatt as he jogged by. Jones, who had access to the county morgue at any time, wanted to take a look at the head to see if might show any evidence of the jagged teeth that had caused noticeable marks on Jones's thumb when Costas realized that he had been rat poisoned by Jones.

Jones had carried Costas's head from the morgue in his maroon bowling bag and was just trundling it with him when he climbed up into the tree. He thought the coconut had given Whitlow Wyatt only a glancing blow and while Whitlow was lying stupefied on the ground below, Jones decided to toss the head at him, too, for good measure. That measure put Wyatt out for good.

You probably wonder about Heidi Hamm and Robert Cleverly. Well, they ended their short affair, with Heidi leaving Key West for L'Ecole Beaux Arts in Fountainbleu, France, to pursue a career as a fine artist.

Cleverly, after being severely beaten up once and wrongfully jailed another time as a suspect in the Delupas and associated murders, has decided that Key West and he don't necessarily work well together.

He was proud of his one good deed, perhaps in his lifetime, of bailing The Viscount out of jail. That was when The Viscount was charged with trying to destroy PrideFest, when, in fact, The Viscount was just being his clumsy, distracted self, putting afire one of the grand balloon arbors on Duval by falling into it from his nine-foot unicycle and alighting it with his cigar.

Cleverly has moved to Nubis, Nova Scotia, a small town in the forest near Sydney. Drugs are cheaper and more accessible there.

Ted Obretta has returned to Philadelphia, vowing never to come back to Key West, although basically he liked the Conch Republic a lot.

Pansy Riviera went back to Kito, Iowa, to continue teaching social studies, though still pining for the never-to-come-back Whit Wyatt.

Seamus Fine and Morky Golub still can't believe their old friend Rabbi Otto Blintz was connected to the murders. Always loyal, they had him packed up immediately and sent for burial in a cemetery in the Williamsburg section of Brooklyn, New York. Later, police found out he had made his money in Key West as a runner for baker/drug peddler Costas Delupas. He knew of Deputy Lovie Jones's protection of Delupas and had no alternative but to stay loyal to Jones after Jones murdered Delupas.

The Viscount and McMary have rehabbed the great mansion at the corner of Duval and United and have become the society mavens of the Key West scene. After a ticker-tape parade where all wires in Key West were taken down so that The Viscount could ride his tall unicycle unencumbered through the many streets of Old Town to great applause, a movement was made to name him a Vice Admiral in the Conch Republic Navy.

Many are saying that he has a good chance to become mayor of Key West one day as well. And there are others who declare that, for his deeds, generosity, humanity and downright goofiness, he'll one day be elected President of the Conch Republic, should it ever fully secede from the Union. But first he and McMary Marimba have become betrothed and plan a honeymoon trip to his native Isle of Goda in the 20-foot tall sailing egg that he is having rebuilt.

Meanwhile, Zero Belinsky, the lovable and sexy former one-armed midget plumber, now with no arms at all, has learned to eat and drink with his feet. He takes life in stride. At least he has three more appendages left.

Read these other books by Ron Watt:

- Dateline: UBI
- A Love Story for Cleveland
- The Art of Public Relations (in association with other writers)

To order any of these books, call (800) 932-5420 or visit www.greenleafbookgroup.com